CHAPTER 1

THEY won't like it, you know." Sir Michael Braine folded his napkin carefully, put it on the table, and stared down the hall.

"The young men won't mind, Master. In fact, they'd be surprised if we didn't go about it properly."

"Yes, but they're not the ones with the money, Giles. If we're to get a million, most of it will come from the older generation, and they don't like these American methods. Take a man like Charles Mowbray. He might give a lot if he's approached in the right way, but if this fund-raising firm starts any high-pressure nonsense he'll close up completely. And frankly you can't blame him. A man likes to feel his charity is his own work. It gives him greater moral satisfaction—a truth, you will recall, pointed out by Thomas Hobbes."

"Ah, yes," rejoined Giles Brereton, with a smile. "But you will also remember, Master, that Hobbes's philosophy was concerned more with expediency than morality—and expediency dictates a fund-raising firm. If we want a large sum—and we do—we must do it the professional way."

It was Saturday night, an informal dining night at Beaufort College. As only eight Fellows, the unmarried ones, now lived in College and the others rarely dined in Hall at the

1

weekend, it had been decided to dispense with the formalities of withdrawal to the Senior Common Room on Saturdays and Sundays. Accordingly, the Master and Senior Fellow, both bachelors, were left in bleak splendour at High Table.

Braine stood up, brushing crumbs from his waistcoat. He gestured towards an oil painting halfway down the Hall. "The Bishop wouldn't like it."

"The Bishop wouldn't like a lot of things. But he didn't live in the twentieth century and he didn't have to find a fortune to stop the College from falling down."

"I expect you're right. Come and have some coffee."

Sir Michael Braine, a small, portly man with a cherubic face and well-groomed grey hair, had achieved his position through cautious conservatism. The whole of his career, from the time he had won the Bigod Classical Prize with a brilliant synthesis of two apparently opposed views on the Antonine Wall, to his election as Master, when the Governing Body of Fellows had considered him the candidate most likely to reconcile the various factions within their own camp, had been based on the art of compromise. As a young man he had achieved this with original ideas, which sought out an acceptable *via media*; now, at sixty-four, he was all things to all people, a charming, essentially kind man whose recipe for success lay in Walpolian inaction.

Giles Brereton was very different. Tall, spare, almost cadaverous, with a pale, ascetic face, he had an incisive mind that did not suffer fools gladly. He had a reputation for terse lectures enlivened only by scathing strictures on the work of his colleagues. He himself had long promised a major opus on Simon de Montfort, but an austere perfectionism invariably led to the recall of the manuscript and yet another revision just as the printers were setting up the type. Rumour had it that he was now going into two volumes. His eminence as an historian had recently been confirmed by his election to the Dryburgh Lectureship, a tribute of great weight and moment in the scholarly world.

DEATH OF A DON

Sinister things are afoot at Beaufort College, Oxford. While the College Fellows rally themselves to hire a professional appeals organiser to raise money to restore their crumbling buildings, the Beaufort Letter, a priceless part of the College's library is stolen. Next one of the most respected dons in the College is found propped up at his desk with a large dent in his head.

As if this is not enough, another murder is to follow, even more gruesome than the last: a don is found strangled, dumped in a books basket at the railway station. To add insult to fatal injury, the deed has been done with a Beaufort tie. Inspector Barnaby of the local police is called in to investigate, but the case is not solved before several other unsavoury events are brought to light.

DEATH OF A DON

Howard Shaw

·BLACK·
DAGGER
·CRIME·

First published 1981
by
Scribner

First published in the UK 1982
by
Hodder & Stoughton Ltd

This edition 2005 by BBC Audiobooks Ltd
published by arrangement with
the author

ISBN 1 4056 8531 X

British Library Cataloguing in Publication Data available

To my mother

Printed and bound in Great Britain by
Antony Rowe Ltd., Chippenham, Wiltshire

The two men retired to the Common Room, a comfortable, oak-panelled room with traditional leather chairs and a log fire. The only occupant was Norman Duncan-Smith, an octogenarian Fellow and one-time Professor of Music, who had long since retired from active service and was now asleep by the fire, his spectacles perched on his forehead, his stomach heaving rhythmically.

"Dead to the world. He spends more time like that than he does awake. Black or white, Master?"

"White, please, Giles. I take it you'll have a brandy?"

"Yes, just a small one, though."

They took their coffee and brandy and sat down opposite Duncan-Smith.

"To go back to the Appeal, Master"—Brereton never liked to leave unfinished business—"You realise we shall have to decide exactly how the money is to be spent. If we were getting two million, it wouldn't matter much about an order of priorities, but as it is we can only deal with the most urgent items."

"Can't we leave that to the surveyors and architects and so on? After all, that's what we pay them for." He warmed his brandy and inhaled the fumes. "If I remember correctly, their last report suggested that the chapel should come first."

"It will have to be a Governing Body decision, and I'm bound to say that the chapel is unlikely to come high on their list of priorities." Brereton, himself an agnostic, was well aware that the Fellows—the College was a self-governing body —did not include a majority of believers.

"The chapel might be put first on architectural rather than spiritual grounds, I suppose. Even Ashe could hardly oppose that."

"Ashe will oppose anything, Master. For all I know, he will oppose the Appeal itself. He hates the College and everything Oxford stands for. We made a grave mistake in electing him."

"You may yet be proved right. But on academic grounds we had to. He's the most outstanding mathematician since

3

Blyth. The College that starts ignoring that side of it is developing a death wish."

"He may be a mathematician, but he behaves like a sociologist. At least we haven't committed the cardinal folly of creating a sociological Fellowship at Beaufort."

Braine sipped his brandy, eyeing the semirecumbent form of Duncan-Smith on the other side of the fire. "It's only a matter of time, Giles, only a matter of time."

"The trouble with sociology is that anyone can do it. You've only got to count the sewers in Liverpool and you're on the way to a degree, probably a doctorate."

"I had no idea you were so cynical." Braine produced a pipe and prodded it with care. "You're right, of course. It's a poor discipline. But we're backwoodsmen fighting a rearguard action in the academic world—we ought to recognise that."

"Talking of discipline, Master"—Brereton leaned forward confidentially, glancing at Duncan-Smith—"I must tell you that I'm disturbed by some of the discipline in the College. I know it's fashionable to say there aren't any rules now, but the Governing Body has laid several things down and they're just not being observed. For instance, there is a rule that women have to be out of the College by one A.M., but it's quite clear to me that it's being flouted in all directions. A lot of women are staying the night just when they want to." Brereton coughed and a spasm of irritation or discomfort crossed his face. "The point is, I find Cowper's attitude as Dean disturbing. It may be that we no longer stand *in loco parentis*, but we still have some responsibility, and if the rule is there we ought to do something about it. Alternatively, we should change the rule."

Braine lit a match and concealed a sigh by exhaling a cloud of smoke. He had heard Brereton on this tack before.

"I was talking to Cowper only the other day," continued Brereton. "He didn't seem to know what I was getting at. I'm sure he's an excellent man, but he only sees the good in

4

people, which may be all right for the Chaplain but is hardly a qualification for the Dean."

"It's a difficult job these days," said Braine soothingly. "When I was Dean just after the war, it was all clear-cut. College rules, summary justice, and no complaints. Nobody moaned because they were all too busy enjoying themselves. Take the gate hours. They were shut at ten-thirty P.M. sharp, and if an undergraduate was out at a party and didn't make it, he shinned up a drainpipe and climbed in through the Bursar's office window. If he got caught, of course, it was hard luck. But he didn't bleat when he was punished—it was all part of his education. And as Dean I only started to worry when the same man was caught too often. That meant too many parties or a rather depressing incompetence. Nowadays they start shouting about their rights at the first hint of criticism."

"I don't say it's easy, Master." Brereton was not deflected by Braine's attempt to lighten the tone. "I know times have changed and now that we and Oriel are the only two colleges not having women living in, it's obvious the rules will have to be looked at. But at the moment this is just going by default. God knows, I'm not against sex and I don't believe it should necessarily be limited to marriage, but these undergraduates are only boys really and we're giving them no guidance on the proprieties at all. Do you know, last week I saw two girls crossing Fletcher Quad at about eight in the morning—they were in dressing gowns and going down to the baths. They'd obviously spent the night in College with someone and there was no attempt at concealment."

"Probably with Muir and Rogers. They never do any work and always seem to be surrounded by girls. Rather pretty ones, actually."

"I mentioned it to Cowper and he said the rule was archaic. Said he remembered far worse things going on when he was up."

"He believes in progress, Giles."

5

"A touching faith. Self-expression before self-control. Rousseau has much to answer for. I prefer the realism of Hobbes."

Wilson, the butler, came in and cleared the coffee cups. A man of limited intelligence but notable reliability, he had served the College in one capacity or another for more than thirty years.

Duncan-Smith stirred in his chair and sank more deeply into it. His stertorous breathing continued unabated.

When Wilson had gone, Brereton leaned forward again. "The day will come when we shall have to take women, you know. I voted against it last time, but the younger men will get their way eventually."

"Women work harder."

"That wouldn't be difficult." Brereton dropped his voice to a whisper and changed the subject. "Of course, if our friend"—he indicated the sleeping figure, now spluttering gently—"were to retire to the Elysian Fields, the College Appeal would benefit substantially. He has no relatives, you know, and he once told the Bursar he was leaving us the bulk of his estate."

Braine put his finger to his lips and shook his head. As a cautious man, he felt such sentiments might be felt but not expressed. "A great man in his day," he said.

"In his day. But an incubus now. If he did have a relative or two, we could put him out to grass in Bournemouth or somewhere, and we could elect another Fellow."

"Of sociology, perhaps," said Braine dryly.

The two men talked for a while longer, then said good night and went their separate ways.

The door closed and Duncan-Smith, blinking myopically, pulled his spectacles down from his forehead. As he heaved himself out of his chair and looked for his stick, he made a choking sound. He was laughing.

CHAPTER 2

THE Michaelmas term was three weeks old. It had been a cloudless autumn day and now fingers of mist were rising from the river and creeping across Christ Church Meadow towards the centre of the city, where hundreds of twentieth-century workers, oblivious of the academic world around them, poured out of offices and cut-price supermarkets on their way to semidetacheds in Botley and Headington. On the river itself the decaying College barges, faded relics of a dead age, huddled together in the twilight, the roar of traffic on Folly Bridge carrying down to them across the water. Beyond the Meadow and the trees of Broad Walk the first lights were pricking out from the walls of Christ Church and Merton.

David Ashe left the weekly meeting of the Revolutionary Socialist Society and wheeled his bicycle across St. Aldate's. His goal was Holywell Street, but with rush hour reaching a crescendo at Carfax he thought a diversion through the calm of Broad Walk and Magpie Lane would be timely.

From his appearance it was difficult to see why Ashe was disliked by so many of his colleagues. Of less than average height, with a pallid, bespectacled face and unathletic gait, he dressed in a nondescript manner and might have been mistaken for an evangelical ordinand from Wycliffe Hall. Only if one looked more closely at the eyes behind the spectacles and the taut line of his lips was it possible to detect the arrogance and determination that aroused such intense feelings among the Fellows of Beaufort. For Ashe was an uncompromising radical, not a socialist or yet a Marxist, but a committed revolutionary dedicated to the annihilation of the existing social structure.

At the moment, however, he was more concerned with Caroline Ferrers than with revolutionary theory. She had been a disturbing influence ever since he had allowed himself to be seduced in her comfortable Holywell flat after a party in North Oxford. For that was how it had been, he saw it clearly now. At the time he had imagined the initiative was his, that for some reason this poised, cultured woman had succumbed to his personal attractions. But now, after living with her for two months of tense bickering, he saw the truth. She had found him amusing in her upper-class way, a curiosity to be caught, tamed, and shown off to her bourgeois friends. The realisation had come slowly, but there could be no doubt about it. Looking back, he saw how she had enjoyed her conquest initially and then taken it for granted; in fact, he had to admit it, while their close proximity had intensified his own feelings, she was beginning to show signs of boredom.

He turned out of Magpie Lane and crossed the High, glancing up at the statue of Queen Anne high in her cupola on the classical façade of Queen's and mentally cursing all she stood for. A bus queue straggled outside the main entrance and he approved the graffiti scrawled on the walls.

At the door of the flat in Holywell, he pushed his bicycle into a side alley, fumbled in his pocket for the key, then fitted it carefully into the lock.

The moment he was inside the door he knew something was wrong. Had he not despised such psychical concepts, he might have called it a sixth sense.

"Caroline?"

There was a noise in the sitting-room at the head of the stairs, an unidentifiable sound. A female voice called back doubtfully, "David?"

Ashe went up the stairs and opened the sitting-room door. An attractive girl stood by the window, her fair hair spread over her shoulders, her eyes wide and dominating her face. She wore a full-length blue dressing gown and exuded a mature sensuality.

"Meeting finish early?"

"No, got fed up and came away. Too much talk and no action. No wonder the Left never gets anywhere in this bloody country." He stopped abruptly. "What's going on here?"

"I was having a sleep when you came barging in. You know we've got this party at the Grants tonight and it's bound to go on into the small hours. They're professional party-givers—probably polishing up their smiles already."

Ashe walked past her into the bedroom. An electric fire was burning and the room was warm; an expensive perfume hung in the air. The curtains were drawn and the only light was shed by a pink bedside lamp. The bed was disordered and a pile of Caroline's clothes lay over a chair. Feeling ridiculous but angry, Ashe looked in the hanging cupboard on the far side of the room.

He came back. "Did you have someone here when I came in?"

"Now, David darling, don't start playing the heavy cuckold with me. Come here." She held out her arms to him, allowing the dressing gown to open at the breast to show her nakedness underneath.

"There was someone here, wasn't there?" An indefinable accent appeared as his anger rose. "You're nothing but a tart. I'd like to—"

"Thrash the living daylight out of me is the next cliché. And not a bad idea either. The trouble is I might enjoy it.

Remember Madame Houpflé in *Felix Krull?* No, I don't expect you've read your Thomas Mann. Modern revolutionaries are notoriously uncultured."

"You bloody bourgeois bitch, you . . ."

"That's more like it—a little proletarian swearing is more your mark. And now"—she moved to the door—"you can get out, Mr. Revolution. Pack your bags and go. You've no proprietary rights over me. I do as I like." She smiled thinly, a smile that hinted at contempt. "I thought you disapproved of private property."

Ashe took a pace forward and struck her in the face. Her reactions were so slow that he did it again before she could put up an arm. She fell back in the nearest chair, her dressing gown sagging open. As she defended her face, he hit her in the body, brutally.

"You made the mistake," he said, "of thinking I was a gentleman underneath."

⁊

Unaware of the events proceeding behind him, Jonathan Plummer, Junior Fellow at Beaufort, picked his way between the dustbins at the back of the Holywell flat and hastened out into the night. Relief at not being caught *in flagrante* mingled with frustration and a wry appreciation of the humour of the situation. He stubbed his toe on an unseen step, then realised his shoelaces were undone and banged his head on an obtruding door handle as he bent to do them up. He cursed. He was not cut out, he decided, to be a Don Juan.

⁊

Evensong in Beaufort College Chapel on a Monday was not an inspiring occasion. Attendance was sparse at the best of times—with the exception of Founder's Day, when an appearance in chapel was a statutory prerequisite to a share of the Feast that followed—and Monday evening, when the choir was excused, was the thinnest of all. Quentin Luffman, the young and recently appointed chaplain, surveyed the congregation with gloom.

Two begowned Fellows sat in the rear stalls: James Cranston, fleshy and rotund, the dome of his bald head reflecting the candlelight and concealing the encyclopaedic knowledge of the Fitzroy Professor of Philology; and Duncan-Smith, grey, strangely unwrinkled, and already apparently asleep. In the front pews were half a dozen undergraduates, of whom one was hardly a volunteer, having been deputed to read the lessons. Farther down, in seats reserved for the public, two old ladies shepherded an even older man up an awkward step and settled him into a pew. Up in his loft, remote and guarded by baroque cherubs, the Organ Scholar improvised on a secular theme he hoped no one would recognise.

Luffman looked up at the roof. Above his head the fan vaulting was given additional clarity and depth by the candlelight; in the farther corners the delicate tracery faded into shadow. There was nothing to indicate the decay of wood and stone threatening the existence of the whole building.

The organ came to a peremptory halt and Luffman, large and fair-haired, more like a rugger blue than a chaplain, started the service. But his mind was not on the business in hand. Although his clear, high voice was soon leading the General Confession, he was thinking of something totally different; of two things, in fact—the College Appeal and Ashe.

The Appeal posed a moral problem. As a priest newly arrived from an East End parish, he believed in a church of people rather than stone, and if a large sum of money were to be raised he would rather see it spent on the needy than on the restoration of a building, however beautiful. On the other hand, he could not ignore the aesthetic claims of the chapel—he looked up again at the vaulting and then down at the Perpendicular windows—and it must surely be his duty to see it gained its fair share when opposed by the rival claims of the deathwatch in the library, the dry rot in the Master's

11

Lodge and the Bursar's plan for the modernisation of the medieval kitchens. If only he could believe that restoration would increase the congregation . . .

An undergraduate, a youth with a shock of wiry hair, got up to read the lesson. Unashamedly, Luffman continued his meditation.

Of course, he realised that the apathy towards the chapel was merely a reflection of the attitude in society at large. But in a small community he felt he ought to be able to do something about it. The trouble was that people like Ashe . . . Ashe. He was bound to come round to him in the end. And as he thought of Ashe a great well of bitterness opened inside him. It was not that Ashe had shown nothing but contempt for him. *That* he could understand, and he thought his Christian charity could cope with it. No. It was his seeming enmity to everything the Church tried to stand for—tolerance, freedom, individual responsibility, simple goodness. Luffman could see his malign influence eating away the principles of several immature undergraduates attracted by his universal iconoclasm. That Luffman could not forgive.

The lesson ended; the reader sat down. Across the aisle, Cranston was looking at him disapprovingly, as though he detected his lack of concentration.

He stood up for the Creed. "I believe in God, the Father Almighty . . ." To himself he said, *"and I renounce the Devil and all his works."*

CHAPTER 3

THE library of Beaufort was one of the glories of eighteenth-century Oxford. Unlike the chapel, which at various times had been garnished with baroque, rococo, and Victorian-Gothic additions, the library maintained its original unity intact. Conceived by Hawksmoor and executed by one of his more gifted pupils, it combined elegance with practicality, twin characteristics of the age that believed in the perfectibility of man. But now the rafters beyond the superb stucco ceiling were riddled with decay and its outer stonework, shaken by passing traffic and blackened by atmospheric pollution, was crumbling away. On all sides it was recognised as a leading contender for the proceeds of the Appeal.

On this particular evening, the same that witnessed the scene in Caroline Ferrers's flat, Giles Brereton, who was Librarian as well as Senior Fellow, was waiting near the entrance, checking in a pile of returned books and saying good night to the handful of undergraduates who had been working in the library until it closed. He was expecting the Bursar, who had promised to inspect some newly discovered damp in the stack-room beneath the main hall.

The College clock, floodlit in a small round tower over the lodge, struck ten with that attractive timbre which, to

13

the initiated, distinguishes all Oxford clocks and bells. The Bursar, Group Captain Guy Farquhar, hurried from the Senior Common Room, crossed the front quadrangle, and approached the library through the cloisters. Of medium height, but spare and athletic even in middle age, his face dominated by a high-bridged nose, he was noted for instant and unimaginative decisions. His one donnish characteristic was an inability to control his children, of whom, consequently, there appeared an inordinate number. He pushed the main door open, and it swung to behind him, making a loud double click as the catch connected.

"That lock's needed attending to for years, Bursar," said Brereton. "It makes that devastating noise every time anyone comes in."

Farquhar grunted noncommittally. He did not understand the academic search for silence, and he knew from experience that a formal request to inspect one item needing repair usually meant a conducted tour of a variety of other disorders. He was adept at sidestepping the additions.

Brereton led the way down the length of the library, past the discreet bays where the reading lamps were now turned out. At the far end a light was still burning, illuminating Augustus G. Wolfe, a visiting American, who had recently arrived for a year's study on a Glock Scholarship.

"Good evening, Wolfe. I hope you're finding everything you need?" said Brereton austerely.

"My word, yes! I don't believe you follow the Dewey System, but your assistant has been more than helpful, more than helpful." He spoke slowly, the light glinting on his rimless spectacles. "I must say that this year at Beaufort College is a real privilege"—he savoured the words—"a real privilege, indeed."

Brereton coughed with embarrassment, the Bursar nodded, and they passed on to the corner door leading down to the stack-room.

"Fulsome," said Brereton, as they went down the stairs, "but a genuine scholar. Which is more than can be said for the average American academic—or the average British one, for that matter, now that we've become a mass-production industry to turn graduates out in their thousands. Curious this modern preoccupation with quantity rather than quality."

Again the Bursar was noncommittal. His distinguished service career had qualified him to take administrative decisions, but he was rarely at ease in general conversation with the Fellows. Certainly he never felt competent to challenge Brereton's conservative views. But Brereton was fully launched. He had a captive audience and did not mind whether it responded or not. "You've only got to look at the courses at some of the new universities. Take history. They cover great sweeps of time with no detailed analysis at all. Renaissance to Industrial Revolution in six superficial lectures—they're as corrupting for the lecturers as they are for the students. There's more genuine scholarship in the sixth form of a good grammar school. As long as we have a few grammar schools, of course. The mediocre brigade will soon—"

Farquhar nodded and pointed to a dark stain on one of the walls. "That the damp you mean?"

"Yes. If you look just here"—Brereton eased himself round an awkwardly placed bookcase—"you can see it spreading upwards. And look at the books." He pulled out a leather volume and dusted off an encrustation of mould. "Aeschylus is suffering."

The Bursar had nothing to say on Aeschylus but was prepared to expatiate at length on damp courses, or lack of them, and the complications of eighteenth-century brickwork. Feeling on home ground, he went on to a discursive survey of the condition of the College in general and the problems of his own Works Department in particular, an organisation always short of manpower and notorious for its employment of the halt, the lame, and the downright incompetent.

Brereton, who had heard it all before, eyed the damp patch gloomily. It would be with him for some time to come.

Ashe returned to the College carrying his belongings from the Holywell flat in a suitcase. He was angry, and the brutal treatment of his mistress had done nothing to mollify him. He passed Cowper, the one Fellow for whom he had any time at all, without speaking and stared at the porter in the Lodge who wished him a courteous "Good night, sir." "Serf," he muttered. "Don't touch your forelock to me." At the bottom of the staircase in Beauchamp Quad he stopped to take a letter off the green baize message board and was about to open it when he became aware of the Master approaching. He had been dining with the Wykeham Society and was wearing a dinner jacket and smoking a cigar.

"Hullo, Ashe. Been away for the weekend?"

Ashe put the letter away unopened and pushed his hands into his pockets, a routine action when speaking to those he wished to shock. "No," he said. "I've just come back from two months with a woman in Holywell."

Braine was unperturbed. "Good. It's always better having the Fellows in College. The undergraduates like us to be accessible, and it helps the College spirit if we're seen around. Half the trouble these days is that so many of us are married and submerged by families in North Oxford. There was a lot to be said for the old monastic ideal." His eyes were humorous and kindly behind a haze of cigar smoke. "As a matter of fact, I'm glad I've caught you. How do you think we should allocate the money from this wretched Appeal? There's bound to be a wrangle when we have a formal meeting of the Governing Body. It will save time if I have some ideas of what the Fellows think before we have our formal meeting."

16

"Do what you like. I shan't be coming anyway. It's the Establishment preserving itself whatever you do. This College —Oxford—it's part of the whole bloody corrupt system. Its elitism sickens me and as far as I'm concerned it can fall down, the quicker the better."

"So you've no strong views?"

"None," said Ashe, whose limited sense of humour missed the irony of Braine's tone. "Spend the money how you like." He picked up his case. "You can put my vote towards the chapel. It's the most fossilized part of the whole medieval farce. I'll support anything that makes it look more ridiculous—if that's possible."

Braine watched him climbing the stairs. He was not upset by the personal rudeness, which he was used to, but he was disturbed by Ashe's attitude towards the College. Not that there was much he could do about it; once a Fellow had passed two probationary years he could be removed only with a long legal wrangle, which was bound to mean a public scandal. It was a problem . . .

Professor Cranston returned to his rooms after dinner. Half-way up the stairs, he heard the telephone ringing, but it made no difference to his measured progress. It was still ringing when he reached the sitting-room.

"Hullo?"

There was no reply.

"Hullo? Cranston speaking."

Again, there was no reply; just the live acoustic of an open line. Then, after a few seconds, the receiver was put down at the other end.

Cranston grunted. He'd had several calls like this recently. A ring, often lengthy and determined if he ignored it, a silence, and then the cutting off. He had almost reached the point of refusing to answer or of saying something obscene before putting down the receiver himself. It was all quite pointless, but he realised it was beginning to get on his nerves. And it was raising questions in his own mind. Who might want to persecute him in this way? Was it just silly games, or was there something more sinister? Was it happening to anyone else? He found himself investing it with an importance it did not deserve.

He was still thinking about it when he started to undress. As he bent, breathlessly, for he was overweight, to take off his shoes, an idea occurred to him he had not considered before. He was just mulling it over when he was interrupted.

The telephone rang again.

Brereton and Farquhar returned to the main library up the small circular stairs from the stack-room. They had spent some time downstairs and the long high-ceilinged hall was dark and silent. The end bay where Wolfe had been working was deserted.

Brereton turned on one of the central lights. "There is just one other thing, Bursar. I've been having trouble with the lock on the showcase. The key turns, but it doesn't always catch."

At the far end of the library, strategically placed by the door so that it could be seen by visitors without disturbing readers, was a glass showcase in which were displayed some of the most prized items of the College collection. At the moment it contained a copy of Speed's *Theatrum Imperii Magnae Britanniae*, which had belonged to James II, a Great Bible signed by Thomas Cromwell, and, in pride of place, mounted on a dark green velvet background and covered by glass, the only extant letter of Cardinal Beaufort, founder of the College.

"Look, I'll show you." Brereton put his key in the lock. "Yes, it's happened again."

As this defect involved security, it was a concern Farquhar more readily understood. "I'll send a carpenter over first thing in the morning, Brereton. How long has it been like this?" His brusque tone managed to imply negligence that it had not been reported before.

Brereton did not reply. He had relocked the case and was standing in front of it looking down at the exhibits. His pale face was lined with a tension Farquhar had not seen before; shock was mingled with incredulity. He pointed. "Look," he said. "Look at that."

Farquhar looked. The glass covering the Beaufort letter had been shattered. From a small, starlike indentation in the right-hand corner a series of cracks radiated in all directions. Several fragments had actually fallen off the mounting and were scattered round the showcase. But the glass did not matter; it was after all only protecting the letter underneath. Or it had been. The letter was no longer there.

CHAPTER 4

JULIAN COWPER was an Anglo-Saxon scholar of distinction who had been appointed Dean in the hope that his liberal views might help the College authorities understand and contain the uncertain aspirations of undergraduate agitation. In the event he found himself in an unenviable situation, caught between the crossfire of reform and reaction. Rebellious students looked on him as a bogus radical who agreed with what they said and then returned to the sybaritic rites at High Table with unabashed complacency; conservatives like Brereton and Cranston considered him a Trojan horse to be viewed with suspicion at all times. Outside the College, Cowper was something of a public figure. He had been associated with several popular historical series on television and was one of those fashionable dons whose opinion is sought whenever an academic view is felt necessary by the news media. His greying hair—premature, for he was only forty—and full face, creased by a seemingly permanent smile, were almost as familiar in the back streets of Bolton as in the cloisters of Beaufort.

On the morning after the loss of the letter Cowper returned from breakfast to find Brereton outside his study door. He waved aside Cowper's preliminaries as they went inside and declined to sit down.

"This is important, Cowper. The Beaufort letter's been stolen."

"When?" The Dean's normal loquaciousness was affected by his colleague's terseness.

"Yesterday evening. Almost certainly some time between ten and eleven. I was actually in the library, down in the stack-room with Farquhar. I'm more or less certain it hadn't been interfered with when I arrived, but it had gone when we came up."

"Nothing else?"

"It's awkward, Cowper." Brereton fingered his nose and coughed. "Wolfe was working in the library when we went down—he'd gone later." He paused while Cowper caught the implication. "How much do we know about him, apart from his scholarship?"

"Not much. But he had all the right references from Harvard when we elected him and, as you say, he's a well-known scholar in his own field."

"The manuscript would fetch a lot of money."

"If it could be sold."

"There's always a market for something like that if you can find it—particularly in America."

"It's tricky. What do you think we should do?"

Brereton was characteristically forthright. "I shall tell the Master and eventually we shall have to tell the police. In the meanwhile I think you should have a word with Wolfe. I could see him myself, but you know him better than I do and you can probably do it more tactfully. Americans always treat me with too much respect, like an ancient monument." He smiled briefly. "I don't think we should tell anyone else for the time being."

"Was it easy to take?"

"Easier than it should have been. The showcase has only a simple lock and that had been forced. But the main lock was on the library door from ten o'clock when it closed, and there was no sign of interference with that. No undergraduate could have got in unless he'd stolen a key."

"Unless he was hiding inside when you put the lock on. It would be easy enough to get out if he was inside already."

"That's a possibility. But in that case Wolfe would probably have heard something."

"Back to Wolfe."

"Exactly. But we mustn't jump to conclusions, and it's quite possible somebody else came in after he'd left. All the same, I think you should see him straightaway, just to see what he says before we call the police."

Brereton left and Cowper stood thoughtfully for a moment by the window. He did not relish the job of asking Wolfe, however tactfully, whether he had stolen the letter. Besides, there were obviously other possibilities. An undergraduate *might* have been in the library; or the manuscript could have been stolen earlier; and what of the other Fellows, each of whom had a master key? And would it not have been incredibly stupid of Wolfe to take it, knowing he had been seen in the library by the librarian? However, he agreed with Brereton, though he resented his organising manner: Wolfe would have to be spoken to.

He found the American in his room stripped to the waist and glistening with sweat. He was, he explained without embarrassment, "doing his exercises." He reached for his spectacles, rubbed himself down with a towel, and put on a shirt without an undervest. Cowper, who for all his liberal ideas was a traditionalist when it came to dress, shuddered at what he considered a sartorial solecism and turned away to look out over the manicured lawn of the Fellows' Garden. It was deserted, but beyond it, in the shadow of the cloister, he could see Luffman talking with an undergraduate.

"That's better," said Wolfe, wriggling his shoulders in a curious way and doing up his cuffs. "Now what can I do for you, Julian?" Among the younger Fellows, Christian-name terms were usual even on first acquaintance.

22

"You were working in the library last night, Gus?"

"Sure. I was in there quite late."

"How late?"

"About half-past ten, I guess. Hey! What is this?"

"It's serious. There's been a theft from the library. Did you notice anything odd in the course of the evening?"

"No, but I guess I wouldn't." He laughed. "I'm not sure what's normal yet. Don't misunderstand me, but there seem to be some pretty crazy things going on all the time. Take that Latin grace before dinner in Hall. There'd be a riot if they tried that one back in the States. And that butler, Wilson. He offers me a charcoal biscuit every night after dinner and I think he expects me to *eat* it. Now tell me. What's been stolen?"

"The Beaufort letter—you remember I showed it to you on your first day here."

Wolfe raised his eyebrows. Cowper thought he was going to make a conventional whistle of surprise, but he refrained. "It was there when I went into the library at about nine. I remember glancing at it as I walked past the showcase. But I didn't look on the way out."

"That helps. It confirms Brereton's idea that it was still there when he arrived at ten. Did anyone else come in after he and the Bursar had gone down to the stack-room?"

"Someone did, but I didn't see who it was. I was up at the far end and he didn't come down there. It must have been a Fellow, I suppose. I understand it's closed to the students at ten. One of them was complaining to me about it."

"Yes. Brereton put the lock on at ten. Now you left at about half-past ten. You can't be more precise?"

"No, I can't." He spoke vaguely, as though preoccupied with a disturbing idea. "Look, I hope no one's got the wrong idea about me. I assure you I had nothing to do with it, nothing at all."

Cowper was placatory, his smile ready. "Of course not. But it does seem that you were around at the critical time and we thought we ought to ask one or two questions before the police do. Did you, perhaps, see anyone outside the library when you left?"

Wolfe still looked worried. "No—yes—the old guy, what's his name—Duncan-Smith? He was in the cloister, going very slowly with his stick. And he was making a sort of sucking noise as though he was chewing gum, though I don't suppose he was."

"Senile decay—we all come to it. He still asks me who I am from time to time and I've been a Fellow for seventeen years. Even so, he gets about, but I can't imagine. . . . Anyone else?"

"No, I don't think so." He held up an admonitory finger. "Wait, I tell a lie, Julian, I tell a lie. On the way past the Hall, by that place where the students buy beer before dinner—?"

"The Buttery."

"Ah, the Buttery. Yes, by the Buttery I bumped into the mathematician with glasses. What's his name?"

"Ashe."

"Ah, yes, Ashe. He was walking in the general direction of the library. But, of course, he could have been going other places as well."

"Ashe," said Cowper quietly. "I could believe anything of him—anything at all."

"I can't accuse anyone, Julian. I didn't see anything that could be used as evidence."

"The police must be the judges of that, Gus. But don't worry about this business. There's no reason why it should concern you, and it mustn't interfere with your work. Please remember that you are our guest here—it just happened that you were around last night."

Cowper smiled the television smile known to thousands and excused himself. As he went down the stairs, he muttered to himself, "Ashe—I wonder. If it was, he's done for himself this time."

24

At night, illuminated by subdued lighting, the Senior Common Room was a restful place, its maroon curtains, oil paintings of former Masters, and dark furniture conveying a sense of calm dignity; by day, however, when sunlight cut through the dusty windows to reveal threadbare patches in the Axminster and the faded brocade of the curtains, it gave an impression of decay. Only briefly did it come to life, after lunch, when the Fellows took coffee there. And even then there was a marked contrast between the dull chink of coffee cups and desultory turning of newspapers and the formal splendours of silver and cut glass in the evening.

On this occasion the dons dispersed quickly, some to tutorials, others to play bowls in the Fellows' Garden. Soon only four were left—Cranston and Farquhar, discussing the ethics of the bombing of Dresden; Ashe, reading a magazine; and Duncan-Smith, asleep.

Cranston, a brilliant but lonely man, had imposed himself on Farquhar, who had been a Lancaster pilot on the Dresden raid.

"I find it impossible," he was saying pontifically, "to justify the Dresden affair on any grounds whatsoever. After all, the Allies claimed to be defending the principles of civilisation. Not," he hastened to add, "that I blame those who took part. It was the policy decision."

"It was war," replied Farquhar.

"Killing more than a hundred thousand in a holocaust? Destroying the Frauenkirche and the Georgenschloss?"

"That's the advantage of hindsight. It wasn't how it seemed at the time. I don't think any of us enjoyed it, but I doubt if anyone in the squadron thought it wrong."

"The war machine had taken over, and when that happens everyone's conscience is ossified. This was a calculated decision to destroy a city at a time when the war was virtually won."

Farquhar replied with quiet dignity, "We didn't start it, they did. Peace is complex because it allows for morality, war is simple because it does not. My father was killed and my mother was crippled during the bombing of Coventry. When we bombed Germany we were fighting to destroy something that was evil."

"Other mothers and fathers? Indiscriminate killing?"

"That's not the way it *seemed*, Cranston. You were in Intelligence, weren't you? Now don't misunderstand me, but you were rather remote from the firing line and it wasn't exactly kill or be killed. When we flew over Europe our lives were at stake. Oddly enough, though I flew more than sixty missions, I only once saw a plane from my own squadron shot down, and that was on the way back from Dresden. It was a Lancaster flying just ahead of me in the bomber stream. Flack got it and an engine caught fire. At first it flew on, losing a bit of height but still standing a chance of getting home. Then, quite suddenly, it heeled over and lost a wing. The crew hadn't a chance and I watched it fall in an arc of fire until it finally exploded somewhere down in Saxony. I knew all of them in that plane. They were not wicked men, and they died believing they were helping to win a just war. The bombing of Dresden was simply another stage in the defeat of an enemy who had long before dictated the terms in which the war was to be fought."

Cranston inclined his massive head. "Forgive me. I did not wish to impugn your motives or those of your fellow pilots. But I believe there *is* a morality in war, though it is sometimes hard to find. I think Dresden was wrong, just as Hiroshima and Nagasaki were wrong, because they were not needed."

"Do you disapprove of the nuclear deterrent?"

Cranston smiled. "No. It's a question of necessity. Freedom has to be defended and the nuclear bomb is probably the only way."

"With indiscriminate killing—overkill?"

"Unhappily, yes. I hope you don't think me inconsistent."

Ashe put down his magazine on a sidetable. He stood up, pushed his hands into his pockets, and moved quietly over to Cranston and Farquhar. Thrusting his head foreward, he said, "You're both Fascists—bloody Fascists." Then he left the room.

"That's what my friends died for," said Farquhar.

Cranston, eyes hooded characteristically, leaned forward. "You know, Farquhar, we shall have to do something about that young man."

CHAPTER 5

O XFORD spawns societies with a liberality that does more credit to undergraduate enthusiasm than to discretion. Many vanish without trace after a term or two when their founding fathers find other distractions, but from time to time one takes root in the shifting student soil and a society passes on to posterity.

Like all Colleges, Beaufort has its share of the ephemeral, but it is unique in Oxford in having two societies whose reputations go beyond its own walls. Of these the Wykeham Society is the older, founded in the seventeenth century for the reading and discussion of learned papers. Its reputation is such that literary and scientific figures of international standing count it an honour to be invited. Even the fame of the Wykeham, however, pales before that of the Dunstable Society.

The John Dunstable Musical Society was founded in the nineteenth century by an undergraduate ambitious to have his own ingenuous works performed. Initially he created little more than a coterie of musical aesthetes notable only for introspection and self-indulgence. But an aunt with connections arranged a visit by Mendelssohn shortly after the tour of Scotland that produced the Third Symphony, and with such fashionable support the society flourished. Subsequently other musical lions had been lured to the College—a visit from Richard Strauss before the war for a performance of *Ein Heldenleben* was perhaps the most noteworthy—and Ethel Smythe had written a virtually unplayable work specially for it. Now its reputation was such that although the backbone of support came from Beaufort, it collected musicians for particular occasions from all over the country. It was not unknown for soloists from Berlin and Vienna to waive their fees for the privilege of performing with it.

In his younger days Duncan-Smith had presided over the Dunstable. He had launched several talented conductors on their careers, while a performance of Mahler's Eighth Symphony in 1932 anticipated the Mahlerian box office boom by some forty years. The Dunstable was now in the hands of Peter Rudden, the youthful and able Boyce Lecturer in Music, whose own conducting had already won him a contract with a recording company.

The highlight of the Society's year is the concert given in the last week of the Michaelmas term, and for this Rudden had decided to perform the Fauré Requiem in the chapel. This evening, rehearsing the choir and orchestra together for the first time, he was in good spirits. Earlier in the day the baritone he wanted for the solo part—he had first heard him at Glyndebourne—had agreed to sing, and now the rehearsal was going well. He looked up the nave to the chorus in the tiered pews and felt justified in self-congratulation that so many Beaufort men were taking part. The fact that the performance was to be broadcast had something to do with it, of course, but that in itself was a reflection of the continuing success of the Dunstable.

It was helpful that the Fellows took an interest. Cranston, a tenor, never missed a performance. Luffman, also a tenor, usually took part but spent most of his time lamenting the contrast between the normal emptiness of the chapel and the ranks pressed round him now. Sweeting, a lecturer in Economics, was a bass, as was Plummer, who enjoyed singing but was unreliable about rehearsals. Duncan-Smith invariably came; he sat, asleep for the most part, in an empty pew.

Rudden, a dapper man with extravagant sideburns, tapped his desk; his habitual bow tie was awry after his exertions.

"Ladies and gentlemen, we'll take the opening of the *Sanctus* again. This time I want you to concentrate on the diction. I don't exactly want the King's College sound." He smiled. "Too precious. But we must have the consonants crisply articulated. Let's have the sharp edges of the *c* and *t* in *Sanctus*. And I want those opening bars even more pianissimo. Just remember that Fauré was post-Wagner—I want a soft, sensuous line. Imagine you're singing the Prelude to *Tristan*. It's really a very secular requiem. No Last Judgement here, you know. Right, now let's try it."

Rudden's trim beat led the orchestra into the first bars.

Giles Brereton had an appointment. He left the College at half-past six and within five minutes was being admitted through the front door of a house in the Turl. Half an hour later he was back in the street. For a moment, as the door closed behind him, he seemed undecided about what to do. He stood with his overcoat open, looking at the pavement. He took out his fob watch from his waistcoat pocket, opened it with a characteristic gesture at once confident yet unflamboyant, then shut it without noticing the time. He unfolded a pair of gloves, put them on, then took them off and put them back in his pocket. Eventually, he turned to his left and walked away from the High towards the Bodleian.

There was colour in his face now, more than there had been for some time; he could feel the unaccustomed pumping of his heart. He looked up at the spire of St. Mary's. Odd. Up till now it had always had historical associations—Cranmer's trial, the recantation, the burning outside Balliol—his secular, professional interest in the past. But *now* . . . was there anything of the Age of Faith left, he wondered, for a lonely twentieth-century man?

⁂

The echo of the *Sanctus* died away in the fan vaulting of the nave. Rudden put down his baton and ran his hand through his hair.

"Better," he said approvingly. "Much better. We can get it softer still and I want more bloom on the tone when you get to the crescendo on *in excelsis,* but that was very reasonable, very reasonable indeed. Now we'll take the *Pie Jesu.* I'm glad to say we've got Robin Panton from Magdalen to do this for us." He turned to a fair-haired boy sitting alone in a pew to his right. "Robin's done it with the Bach Choir in London, so it's not a novelty for you, is it, Robin? I'd like you to stand over here." He pointed just in front of the first violins. "Yes, yes, that's it."

The boy, quite composed and taller than he had seemed sitting down, went to the place indicated.

"Right, we'll take a straight run through to start with. Are you sure you can see me, Peter?" He turned up to the organist's seat high on his right. "The crucial things here are simplicity and timing. Now let's try it."

The organ played its first subdued notes and the boy from Magdalen began to sing. His voice rang out with clarity and purity; Rudden's baton barely moved; experienced though he was, he could still be awed by one of the magical moments of music.

"Pie Jesu, Domine, dona eis requiem; dona eis requiem sempiternam."

The voice carried its prayer in arches of sound round the chapel, an invocation of innocence. Rudden looked above the boy to the choir beyond. For some reason he focused on Cranston. And briefly his concentration broke, the beat of his baton wavered. For Cranston, normally the calmest, the most rational of men, seemed gripped by some deep emotion. He was leaning forward in his seat, his face catching the light. His eyes were screwed up, his lower lip, protruding more than usual, quivered grotesquely.

Rudden was shocked. The expression he saw was almost savage in its intensity. He looked again and Cranston was in shadow; the moment had passed. He glanced across to the basses sitting opposite and one thing was plain: Plummer had caught the moment too. His face reflected disgust.

Later that evening Brereton returned to Beaufort through the postern. He didn't want to meet anyone, undergraduates or colleagues. But he was unlucky. As he turned the angle of the library, he almost ran into Plummer going in the opposite direction. Plummer was apologetic, Brereton monosyllabic. It looked as though he might get through unmolested, but as he turned away Plummer spoke again.

"Brereton, have you got a moment?"

"Yes."

"Not here, I think." Plummer indicated an undergraduate standing at the notice board with his back towards them. "Privately."

"Very well."

"Up in my rooms?"

"All right."

They crossed the quad without speaking. As they started up the staircase, Plummer said, "It's about Cranston."

Brereton stopped, one foot above the other on the stair. He looked Plummer in the face for the first time since they had met by the library. It was almost as though he had never seen him before. "Cranston?"

"I've always thought of you two as friends."

"Yes."

"Then I must tell you. There's something wrong with him."

A bitter smile crossed Brereton's face. "You mean he's ill?"

"No, I wouldn't say that, though some might. You'd better come up and have a drink. You look as though you could do with one."

They went up to Plummer's rooms, Brereton dictating a slow pace. Half an hour later when his colleague left, Plummer found himself wondering whether Brereton had taken in a single word he had said.

CHAPTER 6

BEAUFORT COLLEGE was founded in 1442 as the outward and visible sign of the success of Cardinal Beaufort's career. Enjoying all the advantages of royal bastardy, Henry Beaufort was an ambitious man who had played for, and won, the highest stakes in Church and State. Unlike his relations of the next generation, most of whom were skewered in the Wars of the Roses or beheaded on various logs for being on the losing side, he had achieved influence and authority in the corridors of power without being swept out by the draughts that from time to time made them so uncomfortable for ambitious men in a ruthless baronial society. Accordingly, as one who paid lip service to a certain piety and the ideals of learning—he had among his offices acquired that of Vice-Chancellor of the University— he determined to perpetuate his name by the purchase of land on the north side of Merton Street and the foundation of a College for forty poor scholars.

The subsequent history of the College, like other foundations in Oxford, reflected the political and intellectual life of the nation as a whole. In Henry VII's reign a malefactor was dragged from sanctuary in the chapel and lynched by townsfolk in the front quadrangle, an occurrence causing it to be named the Fletcher Quad after the victim. Between the

World Wars an American manufacturer of motorcars offered a large donation to the College in the expectation that the quad would be renamed after him. The money was accepted but the name remained the same, a deception which the Master justified on sophistical grounds that might in other circumstances have led to legal action. A substantial grant of land added to the wealth of the College at the dissolution of the monasteries, and as some of this was in the Soho district of London it now produced a valuable income, much of it accruing from activities into which the Governing Body did not enquire. The seventeenth century saw the loss of the College plate, given generously but unavailingly to the royalist cause in the Civil War, and of the original library, burned down by a Puritan fanatic during the so-called Popish Plot on the grounds that it housed works of an idolatrous nature. The eighteenth century was a period of intellectual fallow with a series of bibulous, time-serving Masters, one of whom kept a pack of hounds in the chapel crypt until an untimely visitation led to archiepiscopal complaint. Recent history had been dull by comparison. An aged Fellow, a brilliant but forgetful zoologist, was winged by a trigger-happy member of the Home Guard at the beginning of the war when his gown, still being worn at dusk after an early-morning lecture, was seen flapping in Christ Church Meadow and was mistaken for a parachute. But, in the main, life had maintained an even tenor, with the undergraduates working harder and the dons busying themselves with esoteric research and the in-fighting of university politics that is the eternal accompaniment of their lives.

It was customary at the opening of the academic year for Brereton to give a lecture on the history of the College to the new undergraduates, and this was arranged to coincide with a welcoming dinner given by the Dean. The lecture was short and the dinner, designed to initiate young men into the mysteries of gracious living, was long. Five courses were provided, together with two of the lesser wines from the College cellar, the whole consumed by candlelight, with a number of dons—on this occasion Cowper, Brereton, Luffman, a chemist called Bradd, and Plummer—acting as hosts. After dinner all retired to the Senior Common Room where brandy, whisky, and beer were dispensed in sufficient quantities to ensure that even the most abstemious undergraduate should not escape a headache the following morning.

The Fellows viewed the proceeding in various ways. Brereton, disenchanted by the modern undergraduate, found it a tedious chore, but normally managed an avuncular exterior that almost concealed his true feelings. This evening he was tense and distracted. Cowper and Luffman considered it a valuable opportunity for the Fellows to open communication with a new generation of Beaufort men, while Plummer, who had put off a further engagement with Caroline Ferrers to accommodate it, shared Brereton's irritation and looked for the first chance to escape.

At eleven the party showed signs of breaking up. Plummer looked optimistically at his watch. He still intended to see Caroline if possible and had told her to expect him at any time up to midnight. He watched a small group of undergraduates edging towards the door and decided he had done his duty. He drained the last of his brandy, excused himself to a youth talking enthusiastically about climbing a mountain, and took his leave of Cowper.

"Thanks for coming, Jonathan," replied the Dean. "It's an enormous help having one of the younger Fellows here to lighten the load."

"Not at all. I only hope it's all worthwhile and helps to make them feel at home."

Outside the door he paused to straighten his black tie. "Poor devils," he thought. "They didn't *look* much at home. And no wonder, dressed up in dinner jackets with a butler like Wilson breathing down their necks, watching them trying to decide which spoon to use for the soup." He looked at his watch again. Yes, if he hurried he could be in Holywell by

11:15. Once again he felt that delicious anticipation in the pit of his stomach.

Plummer had been born out of his age. Tall, dark-haired, he had the tousled good looks of a Battle of Britain pilot. He was that *rara avis*, a brilliant games player who takes a First in Greats with only a modicum of effort. His life had a leisured air about it that contrasted with the dedication of his colleagues. Not for him the intellectual rat race with a Ph.D. and publication of learned articles as milestones towards a professorial chair. Earlier he had played cricket for Somerset and rugby for Blackheath; thanks to a substantial private income, he had not taken up his research fellowship until the relatively advanced age of twenty-five. At all times he radiated the self-confidence a casual observer might interpret as arrogance—and which sometimes was.

He hurried down the main stairs from the Common Room and out into Beauchamp Quad, making for the postern, which would be quicker than the main entrance. It was dark in the cloister, but the moonlight was sufficient to show the lines between the paving stones. Ahead he was suddenly aware of movement at the point where the cloister turned at right angles. There was no reason why someone should not be there on lawful business, but the movement was furtive and it made him falter, then quicken his step.

He was barely twenty-five yards from the turn when he saw the outline of a figure, its back towards him, its arm apparently moving in an arc over the wall. At almost the same moment the figure became aware of his approach. There was a curse, the sound of something metallic on stone, and whoever it was had gone.

Plummer ran the last few yards to the corner. As he reached it his feet began to stick on the paving stones. He bent to look and found his patent leather shoes coated in what appeared to be yellow paint. Then he saw, caught in the moonlight, a yellow stain spreading from the base of one of the pillars; closer investigation revealed that it was spilling from an overturned tin that had rolled the width of the cloister. He fumed at the thought that his shoes were ruined, the more so as several yellow streaks had reached his trouser legs; but even as he did so he was looking about him for some explanation.

He had only to look a short distance. The end wall of the cloister, backing on to the chapel, formed the College war memorial. Set into it were several rectangular tablets bearing the names of Beaufort men killed in the two wars, the whole surmounted by a neo-Gothic arch. Normally the only colours were the red, blue, and gold of the College coat of arms, but now the memorial was disfigured by broad brushstrokes of yellow slashed in random diagonals across the roll of honour. Here and there, where two strokes met, the paint ran down in ugly dribbles. The defacement was plainly unfinished; the first three panels were heavily daubed, the end two barely touched.

"Swine," said Plummer aloud, his disgust at the vandalism merging with anger at the paint on his clothes.

A door slammed to his left. Without much thought he turned and ran towards the sound. His sporting reactions were operating.

The way he had gone gave the fugitive only two means of escape—a door into the rear of the kitchens and the postern gate into Magpie Lane. Plummer hesitated at the kitchen door and found it locked, so he pushed on past to the postern. It was a gamble, but he thought it more likely that his quarry had left the College than stayed inside. He opened the postern and ran out into the lane. It had rained earlier, and the cobblestones reflected the light from the gas lamps hanging alternately on the walls that made the lane seem so narrow. At one end it curved, bending towards the sound of traffic in the High Street; at the other it led straight into Merton Street where a parked car masked the exit.

At first Plummer thought the lane was deserted. Then, as he watched, one hand holding the postern open behind him, a figure emerged from the shadow of the car at the Merton Street end and ran left, immediately to be hidden by the angle of the wall. Plummer let the door slam behind him and ran hard to the end of the lane. He was not sure what he hoped to achieve, but he had always been a man of action, and quite apart from his anger at the vandalism he had interrupted, he was upset about his evening shoes; they were new and, in an age dedicated to informality, had not been easily obtained. He reached the corner and turned into Merton Street. It seemed normal. A few cars were parked by the kerb; a young couple, both wearing shoulder-length hair and jeans and indistinguishably male or female, were entwined together outside Merton; a solitary undergraduate on a bicycle bumped over the cobbles towards Beaufort. Then, through the strains of Dvořák's Cello Concerto, soaring to a crescendo out of an open window at the front of the College, the unmistakable sound of running feet. They were moving away from him in the area of the Beaufort main gate.

He set off in pursuit. Before he passed the patch of light outside he lodge he could see the running figure. It was no more than seventy-five yards ahead and, as a fit athlete, he anticipated little difficulty in overhauling it. Already he was relishing the prospect of the final capture.

He had, however, reckoned without the handicaps awaiting him round the next corner. By the time the road veered towards the High Street down the side of the Examination Schools he had gained a good twenty yards and could see the figure quite distinctly. But just as he reached the Eastgate Hotel a side door opened and a rowdy group of young men debouched into the street, enveloping him in their alcoholic bonhomie.

"What's the hurry, then?" asked a large man, swaying unsteadily into Plummer's path. "All dressed up for a party, eh?"

"All dressed up and nowhere to go," said another, who had put an arm around Plummer's neck to support himself.

"He's got yellow shoes," said a third, whose powers of observation were less impaired than his fellows'.

"Why don't you come with us?" said the first man, his bloodshot eyeballs only inches from Plummer's face. "We're going on somewhere. I say," he said, turning to his companions, "where *are* we going?"

This simple question led to some confusion and Plummer managed to escape their embraces. As he set off once more, he heard one of them say, "Yellow shoes, old man. *Very* smart." And then he had reached the High and his quarry had pulled away substantially. He was on the far side of the road, past the traffic lights and heading for Magdalen Bridge. At the bridge he hesitated, then, instead of crossing it, he turned in towards Magdalen College and down the slope leading to the river.

By this time Plummer was making up lost ground, but now came his second check. As he tried to cross to the Magdalen side, a stream of traffic approached from the Plane and made it impossible. He was delayed for fully a minute before he could sprint across and follow down by the bridge.

The atmosphere changed dramatically. Above, on the bridge, all was noise, a turmoil of cars and light; below the level of the road, under the arch of the bridge, the sounds of the world overhead were remote and the river gave a new quality of stillness. The trees closed over him as he went down the slope, and it was a moment or two before his eyes grew accustomed to the gloom. To begin with, he could not see where his man had gone. To his right, the curve of the bridge went straight into the water; to the left, the walls of Magdalen did likewise, the only possible entry to the College —a low window at the water's edge—being fortified with downward-facing spikes. Then he saw the boats. At the end of the slope, in shallow water and tied to an overhanging willow, was a collection of punts. Two were waterlogged and the others looked the worse for wear, but there was little doubt that this was the way he had gone. As if in confirmation a faint splash carried across the water from the darkness upstream.

Quickly—again without much thought about what he was doing—Plummer chose the least decrepit punt, untied it, and pushed off. Skillfully he swung the bow round and with a number of powerful thrusts on the pole set off upstream. As he did so the moon reappeared from behind a ragged cloud; above him loomed the dark shape of Magdalen Tower, ahead lay the ribbon of river, lined with an avenue of silver-fringed trees. Of another punt there was no sign. Then the telltale ripples, spreading across the water from beneath the trees on the far bank, showed where it moved away from him.

Plummer pushed hard on the pole, then lifted it clear and shouted into the darkness, "I don't know who you are, but you'd better bloody well stop before I catch you." It sounded a futile threat, he was aware of that, but in this strange Stygian dream he could hear the note of anger in his own voice.

There was no reply, only the sound of splashing water—a paddle, he thought—and his own punt bubbling forward.

"Right, you bastard," he said aloud. "If that's the way you want it." And he plunged the pole into the water.

Unfortunately for Plummer, in the moments he had paused to shout, his punt had drifted nearer the trees and the new impetus forced it in under the branches. He ducked down as they brushed over his head. Still crouching, he pulled up the pole and tried to manoeuvre it to get back into midstream. As the pole came up he turned sideways, looking up to stop its end from catching in the branches; but this meant taking his eyes off the front of the punt, and he failed to see a branch protruding barely two feet above the surface. The punt was low enough to pass under it, but when it reached Plummer it caught him just below the knee and knocked him off balance. His first reaction was to lean on the pole, a folly he tried to rectify by grabbing for the branch itself. The punt moved inexorably forward and, as he felt it slipping away from him, he tried to hold it with his feet. It was a vain effort. Feeling intensely angry, yet at the same time seeing the humour of the situation, he found himself lying on his back suspended between the punt and the branch. At neither point was he firmly connected, and as the punt moved away he slipped gently and with hardly a ripple into the river.

Two minutes later he was hauling himself onto the bank below Addison's Walk. His exasperation was intense. Not only had his assignation with Caroline been thwarted, but he also suspected his clothes were ruined. In his fury he almost forgot that the figure he had been following, with its narrow shoulders and unathletic motion, reminded him strongly of someone he knew, someone he hated.

CHAPTER 7

Ews of the daubing of the war memorial spread rapidly the following morning and the Master, showing an unusual sense of urgency, summoned a meeting of the senior resident Fellows. Accordingly, Brereton, Cranston, and Cowper arrived at the Master's Lodge shortly after breakfast. For once Braine was brisk and to the point.

"It's awkward, gentlemen. In just three days we've lost the Beaufort manuscript and the memorial has been defaced. Normally I think we could take this sort of thing in our stride, but it's an unfortunate coincidence and could hardly have come at a worse time. We're right at the beginning of the College Appeal—the Bursar tells me the campaign manager arrives this afternoon—and, to put it bluntly: Who is going to hand over money to a College that doesn't look competent to handle its day-to-day affairs? We couldn't have worse publicity when it all gets out."

"I take it the police have been informed, Master?" said Cranston, his head nodding forward.

"Yes. Brereton and the Bursar reported the loss of the manuscript at the first opportunity, but we asked them to keep their enquiries discreet for as long as possible and it's not public knowledge yet."

"I've taken the broken glass out of the showcase," said

Brereton, who was then overtaken by a spasm of coughing. "Sorry about that. Too much smoking—I ought to know better. Yes, I've put a note in saying the letter has been temporarily removed. Someone was bound to ask where it had gone. But we can't keep it quiet for long if we don't find it. A plainclothesman came and pottered about yesterday, but he wasn't optimistic when I spoke to him."

"Professional pessimism," said Cowper.

"It won't be easy to keep any of it quiet now," went on Braine. "The Bursar's had men at work getting the paint off since six this morning, but it's a long job and most of the undergraduates have seen the mess. We shall have to tell the police about this too, and I shouldn't be surprised if the press haven't sniffed it out already. You know how they love anything that looks like a shot at the management. It's only a matter of time before they get hold of the manuscript business as well and then we're national headlines."

"I'm sorry to be obtuse, Master," said Cranston, "but are we not making matters worse by trying to conceal what has happened? At the moment the College is merely the victim of theft and a vulgar piece of vandalism, for neither of which can we be held responsible. But once we connive at concealment—whatever our motives—we lay ourselves open to something of a scandal."

"I don't think we've actually connived at anything yet, James. We have merely avoided announcing our loss to the world. And it would, after all, be much more convenient if the police could produce a solution before it all becomes public. There is, in any case, something I haven't told you yet. You see, the breath of scandal is not far away whether we like it or not. From everything the police have discovered so far, it looks, if you will forgive me the use of their vernacular, like an inside job."

"You mean an undergraduate or a College servant?"

"Perhaps neither. Whoever stole the letter needed a library key, unless he was in the library when Brereton shut it.

44

Whoever went out by the postern last night needed a key to that, too. The porter shut it at ten—that's been checked—and Plummer found it open shortly after eleven when he set off on his chase. As I don't think I need to remind you, the undergraduates can be given keys to the front gate, on request, but they cannot get one to the postern. The only people who have keys to the library and the postern are ourselves —the Fellows."

"And the Head Porter," pointed out Cowper. "But Barker's been with us for nearly forty years and if he wanted to steal anything he'd have done it by now. No, I don't think . . ."

"Nor do I, Julian. No, it's possible someone has taken the keys illegally, but we mustn't smugly rule out the obvious fact that it could be one of us." Braine stood up, passed a hand over his smooth grey hair, and moved to the window. "The truth is, gentlemen"—he turned to face them—"there is one thing I haven't told you. Young Plummer thought he recognised the man he was chasing last night. He couldn't be certain—in fact, he hesitated to disclose a name at all—but he thought it was our colleague Ashe."

❧

There was a time when a learned institution wishing to raise funds for its own worthy purposes announced the cost of its plans, sent typewritten circulars to its old members and a few others likely to be sympathetic, and then waited optimistically for the money to come in. Invariably the sum realised fell short of the target set. One or two contributed handsomely, a few loyally but minimally, and the remainder not at all. Eventually the plan for a new library or laboratory became a watered-down version of the original dream and to muted fanfares a third-rate public figure was invited down to open the resulting jerry-built annex to the old library, laboratory, or whatever.

Such days have gone; the professionals have taken over.

When money is required today, a fund-raising firm that specialises in screwing money out of the loyal, the indifferent, and the downright disaffected is hired for the occasion, taking a percentage cut of the overall profit by way of reward. Before an Appeal is launched the prospective donors are analysed numerically, socially, and, above all, financially. This means a target may be set that can almost certainly be reached—a circumstance having the dual advantage of enabling the institution to start spending the money before it has actually received it and of saving the fund-raising firm from embarrassing explanations afterwards. In the old days the burden of the appeal was carried on a single sheet, written in sentimental terms by an enthusiastic old member, and slipped unobtrusively into the annual edition of the magazine. Now it is trumpeted forth in a glossy brochure containing coloured plans and photographs, platitudinous broadsides from cabinet ministers, archbishops, and peers of the realm—the eminence of the institution determines the weight of artillery brought to bear—and at the back, complete with a tearout banker's order, a series of suggestions about the size of donation acceptable from one fortunate enough to have enjoyed the advantages of the establishment concerned.

The firm invited to handle the Beaufort Appeal, that of Sands, Bluestone and Flint, a geological triumvirate of proven reputation, had accepted the brief with something less than their usual alacrity. Though undoubtedly a prestige job that could hardly be turned down, it had certain disquieting features. In the first place it was an appeal for restoration rather than the building of something new. Experience showed that a brochure depicting glamorous new buildings brought a more generous response than one composed solely of depressing illustrations of the ravages of time on ancient stonework with a sad commentary on what would happen if nothing was done. Then there was the amount of money needed. Because of the extent of the restoration the sum involved, at least a million, was immense and could not in this instance be tailored to the pockets of potential donors. And finally, the pilot survey of these same donors also gave cause for concern. Beaufort was not a large College, or a notably fashionable one, and few of its products were tycoons in the world of big business. If it was to be characterised, it was primarily an intellectual College with clerical undertones, the latter springing from the Reformation which had given Beaufort control of a number of desirable livings. From the point of view of Sands, Bluestone and Flint, academics in provincial universities or obscure public schools and clergymen in tumbledown rectories were, if not a dead loss, at least something very approximate to it. So it was with some misgivings that the brief was accepted. But once the challenge was taken up it had to be met; accordingly, the board held a special meeting and chose their most able campaign manager to deal with it.

In most instances, fund-raising firms appoint erstwhile military men to conduct their operations; they have the necessary administrative expertise, they can mix socially, and as a result of the reduction in Her Majesty's Forces they are in good supply. Moreover, they usually manage to retain that attribute so quickly tarnished by the cynicism of civilian life —enthusiasm. It was this quality that most distinguished the man chosen to handle the Beaufort campaign, Brigadier Sparshott-Heyhoe.

Sparshott-Heyhoe was lean, brown, moustached, and a man of few words. When first taken on by Sands, Bluestone and Flint for a parole period, there had been doubts about his adaptability, but he had swept through the training course, reorganising it en route, and had since become one of the most respected managers in the business, a reputation based on energy and a refusal to take no for an answer. Thus it was that he strode, erect and bowler-hatted, through swirling autumnal leaves towards the main Beaufort entrance on the afternoon after the paint daubing.

His introduction to the College was unfortunate in that the

first people he met were Wolfe and Duncan-Smith. As he climbed the steps to the front gate Wolfe was just leaving.

"Excuse me, sir," said the American, beaming. "Please forgive my presumption, but that's the first real bowler hat I've seen since I landed from the States. I've seen them on porters, of course, but that doesn't really count, does it?"

The Brigadier looked at him with an air of disbelief.

"Allow me to introduce myself, sir. Augustus G. Wolfe, currently privileged to be studying at Oxford, England, on a Glock Scholarship." He looked more closely at the face beneath the hat. "Now you, sir, must be one of the Fellows I haven't met. I find it mighty difficult to get hold of everyone at once. Would you be . . . ?"

"How do you do," said Sparshott-Heyhoe tersely, retrieving his hand from the American's grip. "No, you are mistaken. My name is Sparshott-Heyhoe—Brigadier."

This time Wolfe stared. "My word!" he exclaimed. "A military gentleman. I beg your pardon, sir, I had no idea, no idea at all." And he stood back as though to give an awed salute.

Sparshott-Heyhoe nodded, as he might have done to a green subaltern, and turned towards the Lodge, where a grey-haired porter was watching. Before he could reach this sanctuary of sanity, however, the cumbersome Duncan-Smith lurched in front of him.

"Come back, have you, Pettifer?" he wheezed, tapping him on the shoulder. "I knew you'd come back to get the Ninth right. Heaven knows what took you off to that man in America. What was his name? He never could conduct Beethoven. Only the Seventh, perhaps. There was a good performance in 1936, I remember. But not the Ninth. Too much drive, too much *push*, no relaxation." The old man made to lift his stick to shake it but was in instant peril of falling down. "Come to my rooms before dinner, Pettifer, and we'll run through the last movement. Can't see the score properly anymore, you know, but I can still hear. Yes, thank God, I can still hear . . ." His voice faded and he lost interest in Sparshott-Heyhoe. Looking about him vaguely, he moved off to the gate humming "Men of Harlech."

The porter came forward quickly, smiling tolerantly. "Good afternoon, sir. Mr. Duncan-Smith's in a chatty mood today. He doesn't usually say much these days, but he mistook you for one of his old pupils—a Mr. Pettifer, a most promising young conductor who went down before the war. Killed at Monte Cassino, I fear, sir."

"My name is Sparshott-Heyhoe," said the Brigadier, with some briskness. "The Bursar is expecting me."

"Ah, yes, sir. I'll take you to your rooms. Your luggage arrived earlier and I had it taken up before lunch."

The porter did something to restore Sparshott-Heyhoe's faith in normality, and he was courteously taken to the rooms that were to be his for the initial stages of the campaign. "And right next door, sir, is the room the Bursar has set aside for your office." He pushed open a door to reveal a room with a sloping ceiling. "There's already a bit of post for you on the desk."

The Brigadier prowled round the desk and looked out through the window at the cluttered rooftops. "Bit on the small side, but it can't be helped. Have to improvise, I expect. Nothing like improvisation. Post already, you say? That's not so good, not so good at all. I hope news of the Appeal hasn't gone beyond the College, otherwise we shall have a False Launch." He said it with capital letters. "Can't afford that, you know. False Launch leads to Failed Campaign."

"Of course, sir."

Sparshott-Heyhoe was not a university man himself and the pantomime at the Lodge had not made him feel at ease—indeed, he was mildly irked that the Bursar had not been on hand to greet him—but with his office before him he relaxed visibly. He fetched two leather briefcases from the sitting-room and unloaded a number of items onto the desk. "Nothing like getting organised," he said. "Now, perhaps you'll give me a hand with this desk, will you, er . . . ?"

"Barker, sir. Head Porter. Of course, sir, though if you'd care to tell me just how you'd like it, I'd have it all done for you by the morning."

"No, no, Barker. If you want it right, do it yourself and do it straightaway. You in the forces, Barker?"

"Yes, sir. Sappers—during the last one."

"Good man. Thought I recognised a soldier. Always shows. Right, now just give me a hand with this desk."

For a quarter of an hour they shifted furniture until it was arranged to the Brigadier's satisfaction. Eventually Barker returned to the Lodge, leaving Sparshott-Heyhoe pinning a map of the British Isles to the wall facing the door. To other walls he had already attached a series of red-lettered titles— "Days to Launch," "Sitrep North," "Sitrep South," "Commanders."

He had not yet taken off his overcoat.

❧

That same afternoon Jonathan Plummer at last consummated matters in the Holywell flat. Later, as he and Caroline lay together in the glow of the bedside lamp, she said, "Johnny?"

"Mmm?"

"It won't last, will it?"

"Why not?"

"It never does."

"Experience?"

"Perhaps."

Plummer nuzzled her naked shoulder and grunted. He had entered this affair lightly but already felt himself being pulled towards a deeper involvement. "It depends what you want."

"I don't know. That's the trouble—it always has been. I

used to think it clever and fashionable to deride marriage, but now I'm not so sure. I thought independence mattered above all and my romanticism lingered longer than most. I still don't want children—I'd be a frightful mother. But I enjoy *this*." She ran her fingers down the inside of his thigh. "I like this *very much*." She pulled away suddenly. "The truth is I'm a selfish bitch. And I'm getting older."

He pulled her close again, running his own hand down the length of her back and over the soft curve of her buttocks. She was pliable to his touch and moulded herself to him. "I think you're an experienced girl."

"I'm not sure I like that."

"It's meant as a compliment. I'm almost a novice."

"A very promising novice." She bit his ear gently. "You know who interrupted us the other evening, don't you?"

"David Ashe?"

"Yes."

Plummer pulled himself up onto an elbow. "I thought it must have been—unless you've got a male harem. The outraged husband. That's a new role for him. I felt a bloody fool scrambling about in the dustbins, I can tell you."

"It wasn't funny, Johnny. Look." She pulled back the sheet. "That's why I wanted the light off just now." Just below her right breast and spreading downwards diagonally to the left was a pear-shaped bruise, dark overall yet vivid with redness in the centre and yellowing at the edges.

The shock showed on Plummer's face. He traced the outline of the bruise with his finger. "I'd have come back if I'd known. I'm sorry." Beneath a calm exterior he felt the stirring of an old emotion.

"I never really knew him. I always thought his radicalism was a pose—calculated exhibitionism, as it is with so many undergraduates. But it's not. I realised that the other night. When he hit me, I saw the violence behind all the talk—there was a callousness I'd never previously suspected." She pulled up the sheet and turned her face from the light. "He frightened me—and I was frightened of my own emotions. It's an easy thing to say, but I think I could have killed him."

"He's not worth it, Caroline." His eyes narrowed. "He's a rat of the first water. I haven't told you much about him because I thought you might misinterpret my motives if I ran him down. But there are things . . ."

"Go on."

"Did he ever mention the name Rigby?"

"No."

"I'm not surprised. If it hadn't been for Ashe, Rigby might be alive and leading a happy, normal life."

"Darling, you're trembling." Caroline pulled him closer. "What's wrong, love? Go on about Rigby."

"Not now. Rigby's dead. He's nothing to us now. I owed him something, that's all. I'm much more concerned about what the bastard's done to you." He slipped an arm around her. "I think I'll kick his teeth in."

Caroline's own tension had relaxed as his had grown. "Melodrama? Pistols at dawn in New College garden?"

"Bloody little ferret. I'm more likely to bash him in a back alley."

"Darling?"

"Yes?"

"I like it when you sound ruthless."

"Sound?"

"Are you really?"

"I've never been tested."

"All women admire ruthlessness, though they might not admit it." She snuggled closer and ran a finger over his chest. "Darling?"

"Mmm?"

"I hate David Ashe."

CHAPTER 8

QUENTIN LUFFMAN fidgeted in his chair and sighed the sigh of a man with whom all is not well. He looked at his watch and put it to his ear; he took out a cigarette and toyed with it before striking a match; he stood up and paced a circuit of his book-lined study. His expression, already concerned, became more consciously intent as someone knocked at the door.

An undergraduate came in, a mousy-haired boy with a weak chin and the beginnings of a beard. He seemed to be trying to hide his diffidence beneath exaggerated confidence. "You wanted me to call, Mr. Luffman?"

"Yes, Malcolm, I did. Sit down—I won't keep you long." Luffman indicated the chair on the other side of the fire and offered a cigarette, which was refused. It was difficult to say who looked the more confused.

"You must forgive me for what I'm going to say," Luffman launched straight in, "and you may tell me to mind my own business. But I've been thinking about it and sooner or later someone will have to tell you, so it might as well be me. That's what chaplains are for." He smiled, but there was no response. He leaned back in his chair and let out a thin stream of smoke towards the fireplace. "When you first came up to Oxford, Malcolm, you were a regular communicant, in fact for the first two terms you were the most regular one of your year. Then, round about the middle of last term you stopped coming. I didn't ask why—perhaps I should have done. But I believe undergraduates are old enough to make up their own minds about religion." He coughed and smiled again. "After all, it was possible that, like Evelyn Waugh's Prendergast, you had begun to have Doubts. If you had, it was up to you to deal with them and come to me if you wanted help. It's the most natural thing in the world for someone of your age to start thinking for himself—that's what Oxford's for. So I didn't interfere. And I wouldn't have said anything now, only . . ."

Luffman turned to the window and stared across at the classical balustrade running the length of the roof on the opposite side of the quad. This was the bit he was nervous about, the thing he had never said to an undergraduate before. Broadhead did not help. He sat with an aggrieved air, like an immature schoolboy.

"The truth is, Malcolm," said Luffman, turning back suddenly, "that I believe you've been got at." He was not pleased with such rough and ready phrasing, but it made his point. "I believe you've been listening to Ashe and his cronies. Now I'm a tolerant man in many ways"—he waved a hand in self-deprecation—"and I never thought I would speak like this of a colleague. But I must warn you that he's a clever and unscrupulous man who knows exactly what he wants and doesn't care how he gets it. Now you know and I know that he's a Leftist, that his dearest aim is to overthrow capitalist society."

"Not an unworthy aim, Mr. Luffman." Broadhead spoke suddenly, running his hand round the stubble on his chin.

"That's as may be. You may think so and you're entitled to your point of view. But before you embrace it too whole-heartedly just let me tell you a thing or two about Ashe. I've seen the way he works and—I'm speaking bluntly now—I think you're too bloody naïve to see what's happening." The uncharacteristic swear word did not seem out of place coming from this big blond-haired man. "Don't you see? Ashe still has the looks of an undergraduate and he still moves in undergraduate circles—societies and so on. But do you know how old he is? He's over thirty. He's always looking for converts—impressionable, idealistic young men, like you. Look at the ones he picked in your year—Burston, Maclaren, and that greenhorn Hughes. Look at the year before—Cranfield, Weaver, and Bryant. It's the same pattern every time: the bright lads with imagination and idealism, but not enough maturity to see what he's up to."

Broadhead was looking at his feet. "Suppose he picks the ones who are intelligent enough to see he's telling the truth?"

"That's the way he'd put it, I've no doubt. But from the outside it looks much more like a set of gullible fools being led to the slaughter."

"You're prejudiced."

"Of course. And so would you be if you could see more clearly. It's an open secret that he's been investigated by the Special Branch and he's got some nasty friends in Italy who've been linked with terrorism. You must surely see that his New Jerusalem has a strong leaning towards anarchy."

Broadhead's attention was caught now, less by what Luffman was saying than by the intensity of his manner. He cupped his hands under his chin.

"Let me tell you something the present generation of undergraduates knows nothing about. Several years ago, in his early days here, Ashe got hold of a young research Fellow and turned him into a devoted disciple. He was an idealistic fool who eventually outdid his Master in nonconformity. The College was tolerant, but in the end, when he joined a commune in London and went right off the rails, they threw him out. Within a year he had taken to drugs and a year after that he was dead."

"Hardly Ashe's fault."

"Ashe set him firmly on the path downhill. He selected

him in the first place, he twisted his ideals, and I don't think it's too much to say that he wrecked his career. Ashe was all right—his Fellowship is secure unless he's involved in a scandal of sizeable proportions. Rigby wasn't. A research Fellowship is only a two-year tenure in the first instance, and there was no problem in not renewing it. I wasn't here myself then, but my brother was a contemporary of Rigby's and he told me exactly what happened. There was a lot of feeling among the Fellows, but not a thing could be done about it."

Broadhead was silent, looking at the tips of his fingers.

"That's the first time I've spoken about a colleague to an undergraduate. I hope I haven't been wasting my breath."

"No, I wouldn't say that, Mr. Luffman. But I'm not a fool, you know. Isn't this the way society has always defended itself against men like Ashe—the calculated smear? I think he's more dangerous to you than he is to me. The trouble is he's succeeding, isn't he?" Broadhead stood up and, for the first time, smiled. "No, I think it's you and your lot who have got to do the worrying. And you needn't be too concerned about me in your professional capacity. I think you can say that I've escaped from my bourgeois background, and as far as you're concerned I'm a lost soul."

More confident now in his rudeness, but fingering his embryonic beard to the last, Broadhead left the room. Luffman's shoulders slumped as he sat down by the fire. He stretched for his pipe on the mantelpiece and found his hand trembling.

❧

Cranston was having a tiresome day. A lecture at ten had meant an overhasty breakfast and consequent dyspepsia, a circumstance in no way alleviated when he found himself giving a brilliant survey of Grimm's Law to no more than five undergraduates. A pupil at noon had prolonged his tutorial quite unnecessarily by insisting on reading, in the face of powerful dissuasion, a seemingly interminable essay, and he had as a result been late for lunch. The afternoon had been filled by an interview with a policeman making discreet enquiries about the manuscript, enquiries that moved at such a pedestrian pace that Cranston began to fear for the safety of the third landmark of the day, afternoon tea. Eventually he escaped and made his way to the Common Room, where he hoped to find sanctuary.

Disappointment awaited him. Tea was indeed there, but he had barely started on the crab sandwiches when Farquhar brought in Sparshott-Heyhoe, introduced him, and left on what he claimed to be urgent business. Reluctantly Cranston made an attempt at the small talk he felt was expected of him, but the Brigadier had no time for such pleasantries.

"There's been a leak," he said abruptly.

"Indeed?" replied Cranston urbanely, looking with interest at the man who was to raise a million pounds for the College.

"Yes—a leak. There are several letters in my office that show clearly that people outside the College know about the Appeal—potential donors some of them."

"Is that a bad thing?" asked Cranston, brushing crumbs from his waistcoat. "Would you care for a meringue? The chef has something of a reputation."

"No, thank you. Certainly it's a bad thing. It will harm the Launch—it's a great pity. It's all a question of the initial impact, you know. Go off with a bang and you're halfway home and dry."

Cranston nodded, but raised his eyebrows.

"Successful Appeals are based on publicity and organisation. Do it well and you're in the money, do it badly and you're in trouble."

"What about goodwill?"

Sparshott-Heyhoe looked at Cranston as though he had asked a very naïve question indeed. "Marginal value. Up to a point we can generate goodwill if we go about it correctly."

"How do you think the manuscript business will affect your campaign?"

"Manuscript?"

"We've lost a manuscript—rather a valuable one."

"Lost?"

"Had it stolen would probably be more accurate. The police haven't made much progress yet." Cranston's pleasure at Sparshott-Heyhoe's discomfiture almost compensated for the disturbance of his afternoon tea. "The press haven't heard about it, but it's only a matter of time. They've been too taken up with the war memorial. I suppose you've been told about that?"

"No."

"Someone poured yellow paint on it last night. It's in the evening paper. I thought you might have seen it."

The Brigadier bore up well. "Not a good start. Not a good start at all. But I expect we'll survive it. It's bad publicity, there's no doubt about that, but it can't be helped. Now if someone murdered the Master it would be different." He smiled bleakly, the smile of one who finds humour a serious business.

Cranston withstood the Brigadier's briskness a while longer, then, pleading an engagement and promising to attend a meeting Sparshott-Heyhoe was addressing before dinner, he escaped back to his rooms.

As a protest against the rigours of the day, Cranston climbed the stairs slowly, but he was still out of breath by the time he reached the second floor. On the landing outside his door he became aware of the telephone ringing in his study. He felt the muscles in his neck tighten.

Inside, he ignored the phone. It went on ringing. At length he picked it up.

"Hullo. Cranston."

Again silence. He was about to put it down when a voice said quietly, "Burgess."

Cranston's eyelids drooped in their familiar way.

"Hullo?"

"Burgess." The voice was muffled and strangely high-pitched. "Burgess. And Rigby. I know about Burgess and Rigby."

"What do you want?"

The line was silent.

"Who are you?" Cranston ran his hand over the dome of his head; his voice, usually smooth, had an edge. "What are you talking about?"

"Don't be tiresome, Professor."

"Wait." Cranston moved to the door, locked it, then sat down at his desk. "Now tell me who you are and what you want."

"You're a hypocrite, Professor, a slimy hypocrite."

Cranston's complexion, normally sallow, was blotchy and pink.

"Why don't you put down the phone? You're frightened, aren't you?"

"What do you want?"

"You're a bent bastard, Cranston." The voice was indistinct, but the words could not be mistaken. "I think the press would like to hear about Burgess and Rigby. Corruption in high places is always good for circulation. For some reason no one ever expects it. But it won't do you or the College Appeal any good. No, it certainly won't do that. And nor will your latest piece of squalor, if it's made public."

Through the window came the chimes of the College clock striking the hour. Cranston heard a click and the line went dead. Down the back of his neck and across his thighs ran the sensation he associated with fear. Fear and shock. Shock not so much from the melodrama of the call—that seemed childish and unreal—but from the fact of discovery. Burgess and Rigby were names from the past, a past he considered dead; a past, moreover, he had not thought particularly important.

Slowly, with deliberation, he replaced the telephone; then

he pulled out a keyring from his waistcoat pocket, selected a key, and unlocked the bottom drawer of his desk. From beneath a pile of papers he drew out a bundle of letters held together by rubber bands. He did not open it but turned to the fireplace and pushed it carefully between two glowing lumps of coal. He watched as it smouldered, flared, and finally disintegrated.

Yet, even as he watched the packet crumble, something was nagging at the back of his mind about the telephone call. There had been something odd . . .

The smell of the burning rubber bands pervaded the room.

CHAPTER 9

SPARSHOTT-HEYHOE'S reputation was based on energy and action. Some time before he actually arrived at Beaufort he had arranged to speak to the Fellows on the first evening. It would give him the chance, he explained, to get the feel of the place, and the sooner the Fellows were drawn into the machinery of the Appeal the better. Accordingly, instead of having sherry before dinner in the Common Room, the Fellows foregathered in the small College lecture room where the Brigadier was to address them.

For the dons it was something of a social occasion. Not only were the resident Fellows there but also the married ones who lived out, and one or two scientists whose obscure researches in the Clarendon Laboratory made their appearances in College so rare as to make them unknown to all but the Bursar, who paid their salaries. To mark the occasion, Brereton—whose position as Senior Fellow gave him charge of the College cellar—had brought up some specially shipped amontillado, which was now dispensed by Wilson and a lanky youth in a white jacket and shoulder-length fair hair.

As the Fellows drifted in, the murmur of conversation grew. The Master was at the front, talking to Sparshott-Heyhoe and Farquhar; beside them was a blackboard covered with a sheet of brown paper. In the front row of seats was

Brereton, head inclined, apparently engrossed in something being said by Gibbs, the Tutor in Jurisprudence; he was smoking and coughing in equal proportions. Behind them, with several of the younger married dons, was Plummer, re-telling yet again the story of his previous night's exploits. In the next row the grey heads of an Egyptologist called Swan and a physicist named Partridge were bent in earnest converse. Though apparently engaged in a philosophic dispute of some moment, they were in fact deploring the price of kippers, a pair of which Swan had with him in a paper bag. In the same row Cowper, who always enjoyed his own jokes, was chuckling in anticipation of a climax he had not yet reached; Luffman was smiling politely, but an acute observer would have noticed that his mind was elsewhere. At the back, between a rotund biologist and a professor of Spanish, Duncan-Smith blinked and settled down to sleep. Cranston sat in a corner, speaking to no one. Ashe was not there.

The Master rapped on a table with a glass ashtray, silencing all but Swan and Partridge, and spoke a few words introducing Sparshott-Heyhoe. The Brigadier stood up and raked the room with his eye, a preliminary he had used for years to establish his authority. Before he could speak, however, there was an interruption.

"That's Pettifer, you know." The voice was unmistakable. "What's he conducting?" Duncan-Smith, inopportunely awake, was quietened by the professor of Spanish, a man with a moonlike face whose own grasp of the proceedings was somewhat imperfect. "It's not Pettifer. It's a man who is giving money to the College to stop it from falling down."

"Nonsense, it's Pettifer, I tell you. I expect it will be Mozart—probably the G Minor."

Braine banged the ashtray again and repeated, "The Brigadier is going to speak to us now."

This time Sparshott-Heyhoe did not pause. "Gentlemen, I shall not keep you long"—he managed to suggest he would have liked to do otherwise—"but I want to get you involved

62

in this Appeal right from the start and your help is absolutely essential if we are to be successful. However, before I come to that, I should explain how the whole thing is going to be organised. To start with, it will all be handled from the College. I am what is known as the campaign manager and although I shall, of course, be in close touch with the Bursar, my office will be the centre of operations—the H.Q., as it were."

His delivery was brisk and clear, in the manner of a man used to being obeyed. The Fellows, more familiar with the discursive style and frequently inaudible delivery of the lecture in Schools, were attentive.

"We are after a large sum of money," went on Sparshott-Heyhoe. "Some of which will come from important companies and some, no doubt, from America. But if we are to get anywhere near the total we're aiming at, most of it will have to come from old members of the College. The success of this part of the Appeal depends simply on organisation, and you must all play your part." He turned to the blackboard behind him and removed the sheet of brown paper covering it. "Here is a map of the British Isles."

One or two Fellows blinked, though whether from disbelief or failing eyesight it was hard to say.

"Now it will be apparent to you, gentlemen, that Beaufort men are scattered nationwide. It is our job to catch them, to enlist their sympathy and interest, and get them working on behalf of the College. Accordingly . . ." He removed the map with a grandiose gesture, to disclose another one underneath covered in a web of red and blue lines. "Accordingly, the country will be divided into 'areas'—those are the red lines—and each 'area' will be subdivided into 'localities,' represented by the blue. The 'locality' is the basic component of the whole operation and covers roughly a county or city. Within each locality we appoint an organiser—I call them 'Commanders'—an old member of the College who may be expected to show his loyalty not so much by giving money

63

himself as by his efforts in persuading others. He will be responsible for chasing up all the Beaufort men in his vicinity—I shall provide names and addresses—and will do his best to get money out of them. Beyond him, in charge of the 'area,' is another College man who coordinates the whole region, reports back to me at H.Q., chases up laggards, and generally keeps his part of the country moving. It helps if he's socially prominent—a Lord Lieutenant is obviously ideal, but JPs, big landowners, even Mayors, will do. Once we've had the Launch it's essential to maintain momentum, and these are the key men to keep it going.

"Now, gentlemen, this is where you come in. Any door-to-door salesman knows that once he gets into the house he has achieved a personal relationship with a potential buyer, and he's halfway home and dry. We must employ the same technique—except that with us the relationship is already there. Your former pupils, grateful pupils no doubt, are all over the country, and that is the relationship we must tap. And we must tap it forcefully. We must catch them and hold them. Not one Beaufort man must escape the net. Now to start with I want each of you to produce the names of a dozen men you know well enough to ask a favour of. That will give us a basis to work on and we can cover the gaps later. I want these names in three days. Three days, gentlemen."

The last words were barked out with such authority that even Swan and Partridge took note. "Three days, Partridge," said Swan. "You've got three days." Partridge nodded sagely and repeated to himself, "Three days. Lists of names. It will take a great deal of time. I'm not sure . . ."

Sparshott-Heyhoe hastily went on. "You let me have the lists of names, gentlemen. I'll plot them on the map and fit them into the overall scheme. As soon as the plan is right, I'll ask you to contact them to persuade them to help us. Coming from you, you see, we get the personal touch, the foot in the door if you like. Once they've agreed—and experience shows that most of them will—we call them to the College for a series of meetings. I'll brief them on how to run their areas and localities, you can tell them how grateful you are, and the College can take the opportunity to give them a first-class dinner to spur on the good work. It's worthwhile sparing no expense on that, Bursar." He turned to Farquhar. "Wine and dine them well. Make them feel important. They'll begin to feel we've done them a favour by choosing them. They'll work harder and feel they're letting us down if they don't. We use any pressure we can.

"I think that's all for now. But please remember we are after a large sum of money, so choose good men—men of energy and initiative who can be relied upon to carry something through once they've started it. Now," he looked at his watch, "if anyone has a question before dinner?"

"Forgive me, Brigadier," said a small man in a crumpled brown suit, a philosopher of some distinction, "but have you considered the ethics of this method?"

Sparshott-Heyhoe looked at the questioner bleakly. "Sir, your College is falling down. If you want it to last another five hundred years you have no choice."

No one else ventured a question and after a short pause the Master, whose distaste for the whole business was hardly mitigated by its necessity, thanked Sparshott-Heyhoe, assured him help would be forthcoming, and suggested adjournment to Hall.

After dinner, Sparshott-Heyhoe had arranged for the Bursar to take him on an informal tour of the College. As he put it, the quicker he found his way about the better, and it was as well that he should see what he was raising money for. Accordingly, as soon as the port had circulated for the second time and the gathering showed signs of breaking up, Farquhar and the Brigadier withdrew, put on their overcoats, and went out into Fletcher Quad.

The wind had dropped and it was now a chill October

evening. The Victorian lights strategically bracketed on the walls had haloes of mist. Smoke from a bonfire in the Fellows' Garden hung in the air. In both quadrangles and in the cloisters brown and yellow leaves from the College beeches lay where they had been blown earlier in the day. There was going to be a frost.

They made a leisurely progress, the Bursar pointing out the salient features of the College geography. They went first to the chapel, their feet ringing on the flagstones, their voices echoing round the empty pews; thence, via a subterranean passage that Farquhar described as a shortcut, to the old kitchens whose redevelopment figured so prominently in the Appeal plans. Next came Beauchamp Quad and, at one corner, the Brandon Building, a recently built residential block, the one piece of modern architecture in the College.

"It would be easier to raise money for something like that than for the chapel or the library," said Sparshott-Heyhoe.

"No doubt. But it's not a success, you know. It's all that glass. Too hot in summer, too cold in winter, and no privacy. It's like a goldfish bowl inside. We put the freshmen in there and then let them move out after a year. Some of them say they'd rather live out of College than go there."

The Brigadier pointed to a Georgian façade just visible beyond the Fellows' Garden. "What's that?"

"The Master's Lodge. One of the most desirable residences in Oxford." Even as he spoke the front door opened, a shaft of light struck across the lawn, and the unmistakable figure of the Master, accompanied by someone less distinct, went into the house.

They crossed the Fellows' Garden, passed the pond with its sleeping ducks, and circled back to the main body of the College through the low arches of Lancaster Hall, the one genuinely medieval building. "We put running water in here seven years ago," said Farquhar, "but they still have to cross the quad for baths. It's odd, but the most popular rooms in College are here."

"No accounting for taste," said Sparshott-Heyhoe, who clearly preferred the attractions of the Brandon Building. "It's very quiet. Are they all working?"

"Mostly, though a lot go out in the evening. It's usually quiet after Hall, unless someone's giving a party."

As if to contradict him, a rowdy group of undergraduates emerged into the light near the main gate and made a noisy, echoing progress along the cloister until they vanished into the Beauchamp Quad.

"And that's about it," said Farquhar. "Except for the library—that's the long building on the far side. I'll just take you in there and then you've seen more or less everything."

The library was closed for the night and Farquhar used his master key to get in. He fumbled for the switches behind the door and turned on the concealed lighting, which illuminated the magnificent stucco ceiling. "One of the treasures of Oxford," he said, "and everything's rotten behind it."

The Brigadier seemed immune to aesthetic attractions. "Is this the showcase the manuscript was stolen from?"

"Yes."

"I'm not surprised. It doesn't look very solid to me."

The apparent silence of an old library at night is deceptive. The leather bindings and the woodwork of the panelling and shelves together produce barely perceptible sounds, giving it a curious quality of life. Even Sparshott-Heyhoe was aware of it, and the two men fell silent as they walked over the Aubusson carpet towards the far end.

"Hullo," said Farquhar. "Someone's left a light on."

Ahead, from one of the reading bays, a soft glow, not apparent earlier, reflected monstrous shadows on the walls and across the carpet.

"Unless it's one of the Fellows working late. It might be our visiting American. He's very taken with the library."

But it was not Augustus G. Wolfe. It was Duncan-Smith. And he was not working; he was asleep, head thrown back, mouth open.

Or so it appeared to Farquhar. "He sleeps everywhere. He just about wakes up when he dines at High Table, but he's usually nodded off before the fish course."

"Asleep?" Sparshott-Heyhoe moved nearer to Duncan-Smith. He bent over him, then brusquely seized hold of his wrist. "This man's not asleep—he's dead."

There could be no doubt about it. As Sparshott-Heyhoe released the arm he was holding, Duncan-Smith shifted sideways like an ill-balanced sack and toppled onto the floor.

"Good God, man!" exclaimed Sparshott-Heyhoe. "What's going on in this place?"

CHAPTER 10

REACTIONS the following morning to the news of Duncan-Smith's death were for the most part predictable. There was, of course, sympathy for the old man, but it was recognised that he had had more than his three score years and ten and that his demise might have been expected at any time. The first hint of perplexity came when it was rumoured that his death might not have been as natural as had at first appeared. The library had been locked after the removal of the body and several policemen had been seen poking about, one of them with a camera. The Bursar and Sparshott-Heyhoe, together with undergraduates who had been in the library earlier in the evening, had been interviewed, and the questions asked about times and keys suggested more than a routine enquiry into a death by heart failure. By midmorning the rumour, worming its way between undergraduates, college servants, and dons, had hardened to near certainty.

"Something's rotten in the state of Denmark," said an undergraduate with a limited literary repertoire.

"It smells to heaven," rejoined another, one of the last actually to see Duncan-Smith moving.

At 11:30 Chief Detective Inspector Barnaby called on the Master to pay his respects.

Barnaby was not a self-effacing policeman. In the first place he was exceedingly tall, well over six feet, and his angular figure, a thing of abrupt joints and unexpected straight lines, gave the impression of being composed entirely of bone. His face, its flesh drawn tight over prominent nose and cheek-bones, was dominated by eyes set in dark hollows. Even had he not been physically compelling, however, his seemingly inexhaustible funds of energy would have made him notable. He had been on the case for only two hours but had already managed to see many of the Fellows and a sprinkling of under-graduates. His mere presence had galvanised the local con-stabulary into greater action over the manuscript, and the manpower had been stepped up.

Now, in Braine's drawing-room, he sat in a winged arm-chair, his knees projecting uncompromisingly in front of him. "Not much doubt about it, I'm afraid, sir. We shall have to wait for the postmortem, of course, but there's a great bruise on the side of his head and there'd been some bleed-ing. Then there's blood on the corner of one of the book-cases, down near the floor. Our first guess is that he hit his head there, but there could be a weapon of some sort."

Braine was bewildered; donnish and urbane as usual, but bewildered nevertheless. "Perhaps he fell over, hit his head, then sat down at the table and died. Is that possible?"

"I can't rule anything out at this stage, sir. But he wasn't sitting naturally at the table and it could be that he was put there when he was already dead."

"The Bursar thought he was asleep."

"Yes, but from all I hear members of the College expected to see him asleep everywhere. The Brigadier had no doubt he was dead the moment he saw him."

"But you're not really suggesting murder, Inspector?"

Barnaby held up his hand. "We just have to be cautious, sir, as I'm sure you understand. At the moment it just looks odd. You see there were one or two other things. The Profes-sor wasn't wearing his glasses and we've found them in the

70

reading bay next to the one he was in. And his clothes were rumpled. There's a button missing from his waistcoat."

"He was an old man, Inspector. You don't expect Savile Row from an octogenarian Oxford don."

"I appreciate that, sir. But I have to be objective in my assessment. And to me it looks as though there was a struggle. What I'm trying to do now is build up a picture of the Professor's last hours, but with so many people in the College yesterday evening it's a wide field."

"The library was locked, Inspector. Only the Fellows have keys."

"It wasn't locked until ten. Several people saw Duncan-Smith there after dinner. The trouble is, none of them knows whether he was alive or dead when they saw him. He *may* have been killed after the door was locked, but he *could* have died before. The doctor's report says any time between eight P.M. and eleven P.M., which doesn't help much. And we haven't been able to get in touch with the librarian's assistant, Mrs. Jarvis. She seems to have locked up as usual last night, but she has this morning and this afternoon off and doesn't seem to be at home. Unless she hears the news and comes in of her own accord I shan't be able to see her before she comes on duty again later today."

Braine approved of the gaunt policeman before him. Sitting on the edge of his chair, he exuded a sense of nervous tension and, oddly, strength.

"I don't imagine you've made much progress with a motive, Inspector? It's hard to credit he had any enemies."

"A doddery old crank is the general impression I've picked up." Barnaby smiled. "If you'll forgive me for saying so, sir, the sort of chap the layman still thinks of as the typical Oxford don. But we've only just started. There are a couple of men going through his rooms now."

"Do you want to ask me anything? I don't think I've seen much that can help, but presumably you want to speak to everyone."

Barnaby made a vague, self-deprecating gesture. "I was leading up to that, sir—discreetly. But since you raise the matter, perhaps you would be good enough to tell me when you last saw Duncan-Smith."

"In the Common Room after dinner. Considering how many Fellows were dining, we broke up quickly and he was one of the first to go. I thought he'd gone to bed."

"And your own movements after that?"

"Well, we were entertaining Brigadier Sparshott-Heyhoe—the man who's running this Appeal you've probably heard about—and shortly after he'd gone to look around the College with the Bursar I went back to the lodge. That must have been somewhere between ten-thirty and eleven P.M."

"Alone, sir?"

"Yes."

"That would take you past the library?"

"It would."

"You saw no one?"

"There were one or two undergraduates looking at the notice board outside the Buttery, but I didn't see anyone else. It was as quiet as the grave by the library, if you will forgive the expression. I remember contrasting the silence with the row the night of the Boat Club Dinner. Most of them got drunk—they always do, of course—and a girl from St. Hilda's was thrown into the pond. No, it was certainly quieter last night. And I remember thinking about the manuscript as I passed the library door. That's been overshadowed, of course, and rightly, by poor Duncan-Smith's death."

"Did you see anyone else later on?"

"Yes. Professor Cranston came to see me at the Lodge—it must have been after eleven. He stayed some time and it was past midnight when he went back to his rooms."

"And you can think of no one who might have wanted to harm the old man, sir?"

"No, Inspector." Involuntarily he added, "Not even Ashe." Barnaby raised his eyebrows. Braine took off his spectacles and folded them away. "Disregard that remark, Inspector. It was totally unjustified. It's just that Ashe succeeds in upsetting everyone here, even me. Have you met him yet?"

Barnaby took out a pale brown notebook and turned several pages. "No," he said. "We've interviewed several Fellows, but we've yet to see Mr. Ashe, Mr. Plummer, and Professor Cranston of those who live in the College. But I shall be surprised if they add much. More or less any of the dons could have gone into the library once it was locked, and there were plenty of possibles before the library closed at ten. There were so many more Fellows in the College than usual with the dinner for the Brigadier."

"So no leads?"

"No. The only thought so far is that if there isn't a weapon and if he did hit his head on the bookcase, then it probably wasn't intentional. Whoever did it—if that's what happened —knocked him over, found he was out cold, and put him at the table. He may not even have realised he was dead."

"But why should Duncan-Smith be fighting in the library?" Braine laughed aloud; the idea was absurd. He turned away to the window. "Whoever did it was a madman. Duncan-Smith was batty but harmless." And then he remembered he was also very rich and that the College was likely to benefit substantially under his will. "But I've thought of a motive and if it's the right one, you'll have one of the oddest cases on record."

❧

Barnaby returned to the library where a forensic team was just packing up.

"Prints won't be any good, sir," said a bored man with a camera. "Everything's smothered."

"But we've found one or two bits and pieces," said Detective Sergeant Arnold, a big, florid man, who had originally been investigating the manuscript theft but had now switched to help Barnaby because of his familiarity with the territory. "There's nothing in the bay where the body was. But I've got the button off his waistcoat—it was over there, not far from the blood on the bookcase. And there's something else. I found this down by the librarian's desk, just behind the catalogue." He held up a black badge, about half an inch in diameter, with the word "Peace" inscribed above a small white dove. "The catch is broken."

"Could it have been there long?"

"The library was cleaned yesterday afternoon. The woman who does it is prepared to swear it wasn't there then."

Barnaby turned it over. "Made in the U.S.A. I wonder about our American friend, Wolfe. He's often in here apparently. Anything else?"

"Only this." Arnold pointed to a shelf of leatherbound books at shoulder height in the bay next to the one in which the body had been found. It contained speeches by Pitt and Fox, and the collected works of Burke. "The first five volumes of Pitt are all right, but in the middle of the shelf Fox and Burke are all mixed up and Volumes IV and V of Burke are upside down. It's as though someone had bundled them onto the shelf in a hurry. All the other shelves are meticulously correct—I can't see one book out of place. Mr. Brereton knows of no reason why they should be disarranged."

"Nothing behind them?"

"No. I thought of that."

"Check them for prints. Then go through the people who admit to being in the library after nine last night. I want a more detailed picture of comings and goings. I'm off to see the dons we've missed so far. I'll take that badge."

Carefully Barnaby dropped it into a plastic bag and left to see Cranston, who had promised to be in his rooms all morning. He found him working at a typewriter; pale sunlight glinted on his head and gave warmth to the mahogany of the desk at which he was sitting.

The Professor was courteous but guarded, as though un-

74

sure of how far to commit himself. About his own movements the previous night he was perfectly clear. He had dined in Hall after listening to Sparshott-Heyhoe. Some time after ten he had gone to his rooms, where he had worked for something under an hour. At about eleven—pressed, he would say a little after rather than before—he had gone to see the Master at the Lodge. He had stayed until shortly after midnight.

"You passed the library on the way there?"

"Certainly."

"And you noticed nothing out of the ordinary?"

"Nothing. I was preoccupied."

Barnaby had the feeling Cranston had taken a private decision, one he had been considering since he had entered the room. He asked what he hoped was the right question, "Why did you go to see the Master, Professor?"

Cranston looked over his glasses; his expression registered a new respect. "A private matter, Inspector, but one I believe I should tell you about. I trust my confidence will be safe when it proves to have no connection with Duncan-Smith's death."

"Of course."

The Professor touched his fingertips lightly together in front of him. "I'm not married, Inspector, and about ten years ago I had a relationship—a special relationship, you might call it—with one of my pupils, a boy called Burgess, a member of the College. Society condemned such things then and in large measure still does. But it was not a sordid affair between a dirty old man and an innocent boy, though to an outsider I suppose it might have looked like that. No, there was real affection on both sides, an affection I have never regretted. Eventually the young man went down, and we saw less and less of each other. I believe he now has a wife and family and he's probably forgotten about me altogether. But I don't forget. Putting it simply, it was one of the few friendships of my life. The trouble is that someone else hasn't forgotten him either. Yesterday afternoon I had an anonymous telephone call from someone wanting to make trouble. That was why I went to see the Master."

"Just because of an anonymous call?"

"No. You see, I realised who it was. Not at first, but later. There was a quality about the voice I thought I recognised, and just before he put the telephone down I heard a sound that was unmistakable. It was the College clock striking the hour. At the time I wasn't sure whether I'd heard it in my room or on the phone, but in retrospect I was sure it was on the phone. Now that meant it was someone inside the College, someone whose room was near the clock. And once I saw that, I recognised the voice and it all fell into place. I even remembered the occasion when he would have realised the truth about my relationship with the young man."

"And who was it?"

"Ashe," said Cranston. "Ashe, the revolutionary hero who once led another young man astray by telling him to fulfil himself by breaking away from the conventions of society. And Ashe had the nerve to try to attack *me*." He flushed with anger, the veins standing out on his temple. "And he was wrong. He even suggested I'd had a relationship with the boy *he* destroyed—Rigby."

"And you hadn't?"

"Certainly not. That was quite different. I just happened to know him well for other reasons."

"That's all he said?"

"Not quite."

"Go on, sir."

"He implied that I'm chasing someone now."

"And are you?"

Cranston took his glasses off with the sweeping gesture familiar to those who attended his lectures. "You are blunt, Inspector. And I will be equally so. It is my misfortune to be attracted to boys and young men. It does not necessarily mean that I do anything about it. Yes, I *am* attracted to a

76

young boy who is singing as a soloist with the Dunstable Musical Society and it's possible—no, it seems certain—that it's been noticed. But I've done nothing, nothing at all of which I need be ashamed. That is what I told the Master. Once I knew it was Ashe, I could see the scandal he might try to make of it and the harm it could do me and the College."

"Thank you for telling me all that, sir. It can't have been easy. Now, can you think of any reason why Duncan-Smith should have been killed?"

"None at all, Inspector. He was perfectly harmless. Infuriating, of course, as senile old men always are, but I can't conceive of anyone wanting to harm him. I can only suppose his death has something to do with the loss of the manuscript. Is it possible he may have suspected who the thief was?"

"There may be a connection, Professor, but it's pure speculation. It hasn't escaped us that there have been three untoward events in the College in a week and two of them happened in the library."

Barnaby excused himself, went down the uncarpeted staircase and out into the pale sunlight. Whatever the possible link between events in Beaufort, one thing stood out: practically everybody had mentioned Ashe and he was universally disliked. The next step was obviously to meet the object of such execration. However, a visit to Ashe's rooms, enquiries at the porter's lodge, and telephone calls to various parts of Oxford revealed that this was easier said than done. Indeed, when it transpired that no one had seen Ashe since dinner the previous night, and when his scout reported that he had not slept in College, only one conclusion was possible: Ashe had disappeared.

CHAPTER 11

WHILE a search was mounted for Ashe, Barnaby called on Plummer, the remaining living-in Fellow. He found him in his rooms overlooking Beauchamp Quad where he had just finished a tutorial. A cloud of cigarette smoke hung in layers across the room, bending upwards towards the open window. Barnaby took in the eighteenth-century prints, the Chinese carpet, and the matching blue-velvet curtains; rightly he judged Plummer a man of taste with the wealth to sustain it.

"Sorry about the smoke, Inspector. Filthy habit, but you've got to let them do it if they want to. Probably lucky it's not pot. It takes me a good twenty-four hours to get the smell out when that particular trio has been in here. What can I do for you?"

Barnaby observed the impressive cut of Plummer's suit, a successful blend of the contemporary and conservative in a fine brown tweed. "I'm interested in anything to do with Duncan-Smith's death, Mr. Plummer. To start with, can you think of any possible motive?"

"None at all. He was a queer old bird and we all got tired of him at times, but as far as I know he had no enemies. I suppose it might have been something out of his past, something we know nothing about."

"That's always a possibility. Did he have any particular friends?"

"Not really. All his generation retired a long time ago—to be honest, most of them are dead. Just occasionally an old pupil came back to see him, but there were no regulars. He was just a lonely man waiting to die."

"Now about last night, sir. Were you anywhere near the library yourself?"

"I came past it after dinner. But then you have to if you are coming up here from the Common Room. It's in a very central position."

"What time was that?"

"About ten, I should think. I stayed for port but not for long."

"You came straight back here?"

"Yes."

This blunt, somehow uncommunicative affirmative caught Barnaby's attention. He pressed further. "And you were in your rooms for the rest of the evening?"

Plummer smiled, uneasily but with a certain openness Barnaby thought he recognised as frankness. "Yes, I stayed in my rooms, Inspector. You see, I had a woman here. I don't want to bring her into all this because she had nothing to do with Duncan-Smith's death, but I shouldn't want to mislead you by lying. We had made love for the first time in the afternoon and I brought her back here in the evening. She stayed all night and we didn't go out."

Barnaby looked more embarrassed than Plummer. "I see," he said.

"She'll corroborate that, but I'd rather she didn't have to. She didn't know Duncan-Smith at all as far as I know, though I expect she's seen him about. He was a familiar figure in Oxford."

"I don't see why she should be involved at the moment, but if we don't make some headway soon I may have to see everyone who was in the College last night."

"I understand. Well, she lives in Holywell, so she's not far away."

"Any ideas where I might find Mr. Ashe? He seems to have vanished."

Plummer raised one eyebrow almost imperceptibly. "No, Inspector. And frankly he won't be missed if he doesn't reappear. As you've probably discovered already, he isn't exactly popular among the Fellows. Now if *he* had been murdered, I could give you about fifty motives, including a couple for myself. However, that's no help to you."

"Was there any connection between Duncan-Smith and Ashe?"

"I shouldn't think so. The old man probably didn't even realise he was a Fellow, and Ashe looked on him as an anachronism, a relic of a dead Oxford—which I suppose he was."

Barnaby took out the badge found in the library. "Seen one of these before?"

"Yes. It's one of those bogus peace movements. World peace and the brotherhood of man on the surface but a Communist cell underneath—you know the sort of thing. One or two left-wing undergraduates have them and, since you mentioned him," Plummer looked appraisingly at Barnaby, "so has Ashe."

"Thank you, Mr. Plummer. That's most helpful."

Barnaby stood up, declined a sherry, and made his way down to the Beauchamp Quad. The problem of Ashe was becoming central to the whole investigation, and if he could not find the man himself he could at least look at his rooms.

Ashe's rooms were in a pleasant position on the south side of Fletcher Quad. High-ceilinged and light, with broad sash windows, they would have been gracious in other hands. As it was, they exuded a bleakly utilitarian atmosphere, the drab cream colour scheme and simple furnishings suggesting the Bursar's choice rather than the preference of the inmate. Only the books on the shelves, methodically arranged, the

80

piles of political magazines, and the large wall posters, dominated by themes of pop and protest, gave the rooms any character at all.

Barnaby made sure the outer door was shut, then carried out a quick but thorough search. He had no idea what he was looking for, but when there was no clear lead he believed in chasing down any alley until it turned out to be blind. The mere fact of Ashe's disappearance was enough to make him curious.

At first he found little of interest; Ashe's affairs seemed as drab as his room. His papers fell into two clear groups: mathematical and political. Of the mathematical ones, some were his pupils' work and some his own, but they might have been Egyptian hieroglyphics for all Barnaby could tell. From the political papers he could see that Ashe had at one time or another flirted with every revolutionary splinter group worthy of the name, displaying an unusual doctrinal eclecticism. Pamphlets, published and unpublished articles, correspondence with secretaries of Marxist, Trotskyite, and Maoist organisations—Barnaby thumbed through them all, marvelling at their dedication. "No sense of humour," he thought. "That's their trouble."

Only two things attracted his notice. One was a magazine called *World Peace*, which had on its title page the same dove design as the badge, the other a photograph of an attractive woman, with the inscription: *Till next time, darling. Caro.* This was the only suggestion of a personal relationship and it seemed to have been pushed to the back of a drawer. Apart from that there was nothing. Ashe appeared to have no other interests, and there was no hint of any link with Duncan-Smith.

Barnaby shut the last drawer, walked across to the window, and stared out into Fletcher Quad. A group of undergraduates, hands in pockets, slouched towards lunch in Hall; in the far corner, beneath the cloister, Farquhar and Brereton were talking animatedly; across the grass, a laundryman headed for

81

the postern gate, a large wicker basket perched on his shoulder. Overhead, the College clock struck one and Barnaby automatically glanced down at his own watch. As he did so he saw something he had not noticed before. On the windowsill in front of him, almost behind one of the curtains, lay what at first he thought was a black button. But a closer look revealed it to be a small piece of wax, with a strip of ribbonlike paper attached. He picked it up and let it lie in the palm of his hand. It was sheer surmise, of course, but there was a faded impression of a coat-of-arms on the wax, and guesswork suggested he had found the seal from the Beaufort letter.

☙

Sir Michael Braine was on the telephone to the press, watched by Sparshott-Heyhoe and Cowper, with whom he had been discussing the situation over post-luncheon coffee. His exterior was as unruffled as ever, but there was an edge to his voice. "No, I am not prepared to make a statement. No doubt the police will do so when there is something to report."

A crackle in the earpiece indicated the persistence of the caller.

"I thought I had made myself clear, Mr. Castle. I don't wish to be discourteous, but you will understand that I am very busy today. Your paper will have to contain itself a little longer. Good-bye to you." He replaced the telephone and turned to Sparshott-Heyhoe. "I expect you know more about these people than I do. Persistent beggars—and only doing their job, of course. The trouble is that they'll print what they want whatever I say. Now, how do you advise we handle this from the Appeal point of view, Brigadier?"

"It's difficult, Sir Michael, I won't disguise that. And we don't yet know how bad it is. If it turns out the old man had heart failure or was killed by an outsider, we'll be able to ride it without too much trouble. But if it turns out to be a Beaufort man . . . The snag is that it all coincides with the

Launch itself. The old members will get the Appeal while the death is still making headlines. And there's still the wretched letter. The press don't seem to have heard of that yet."

"Couldn't we play for sympathy?" said Cowper, smiling characteristically. "Poor old alma mater falling down and being attacked by lunatics and vandals at the same time. After all, it's hardly our fault if . . ."

"We don't know whose fault it is, Julian. That's the trouble," said Braine, ignoring the other's facetious tone. "If Plummer is to be believed, Ashe was responsible for the paint, so it's just as likely that someone here stole the letter and killed Duncan-Smith."

"What do you want me to do about Ashe, Master?" asked Cowper. "Presumably someone will have to tackle him about the war memorial. Do you want me to do it? I don't mind, but you know he regards me as a pallid liberal and therefore infinitely more suspect than a hardened reactionary."

"No, I'll do it. And if he admits it, the whole question of his Fellowship will have to be raised before the Governing Body. It's all most distasteful."

"He'll fight the College all the way. I wonder if we wouldn't be wiser to contain him as we have done so far. After all, no one was hurt by the paint daubing. One might even consider it a piece of eccentricity in the Oxford tradition."

Braine shook his head; Sparshott-Heyhoe looked on disapprovingly but realised it was not his place to comment. Before either of them could speak, however, there came a knock at the door and, in response to the Master's invitation, Brereton and Farquhar came in. Both men were agitated, Brereton coughing and looking more strained and ascetic than usual.

"The worst has happened, Master," said Brereton.

"I won't try to guess, Giles. What has happened?"

"The letter has been destroyed."

"It was always a possibility. How do you know?"

"The remains were sent to me this morning," interposed Farquhar. "They arrived with the second post," he added inconsequently.

Brereton held out a cheap foolscap envelope and emptied it onto Braine's desk. Fragments of parchment, dry and brown, fell onto the blotter.

"There's no doubt?"

"None at all."

They stood in a circle around the small pile of torn remnants, like Druids awaiting some incantation. Brereton's sense of loss and outrage had communicated itself to them all, and, shockingly, as they realised afterwards, the destruction of the letter briefly eclipsed Duncan-Smith's death.

"It's just been ripped up, torn to shreds." Brereton, not normally given to the waste of words, descended to a statement of the obvious.

Characteristically, Braine accepted the news with sangfroid. He picked up the envelope. "Typed. The police may be able to find the machine. But there's no stamp. I thought it came with the post?"

"It did. It must have been slipped in with the normal post before it reached my office. You know what that means."

"An inside job," said Sparshott-Heyhoe gloomily. "If we're not careful the Appeal is going to be ruined."

CHAPTER 12

BARNABY climbed the stairs to the eyrie
that was Sparshott-Heyhoe's campaign office; he
had already decided that his curiously jointed legs had not
been designed with the Oxford staircase system in mind.

"I wanted a quiet word, Brigadier," he opened, when he
had inserted himself into a chair wedged in the small space
between the desk and the window. "You and I are both out-
siders and can be objective. Although you haven't been here
more than a few hours longer than I have, they do include
the hours of the Professor's death. Besides, you've seen these
people in their social context. I've only met them when
they're wary and on their guard. In short, Brigadier, I should
be grateful for your help."

"Certainly, Inspector. I'll do all I can, though I'm bound
to say that I doubt if my contribution is likely to be mo-
mentous. Quite apart from your side of it, I want this whole
business cleared up as soon as possible so that it doesn't foul
up the Appeal. It's bad enough already." He looked gloomily
at the chart headed "Days to Launch."

"Good. Now to start with, have you noticed any tensions,
any odd personal feelings I ought to know about? For example, have you spotted any dislike of Duncan-Smith?"

"No, I can't help you there. There's been the odd bit of
irritation, but everyone I've spoken to is mystified."

"Yes, that's my impression. What do you make of Ashe?"

"Can't help you much with him, either." Sparshott-Heyhoe spoke in clipped phrases. "I met him briefly yesterday in Hall—he didn't come to my talk about the Appeal, I gather. The Master even suggested he might try to sabotage it. I haven't met anyone with a good word to say for him, but I don't suppose you have either. Plummer thinks he was responsible for the paint business."

"What about the others?"

The Brigadier, whose respect for Barnaby was growing, pulled back his shoulders. "Anything I say must be treated in the strictest confidence. I should have said that before."

"Of course. Off the record."

"The Master is competent, but freewheeling into retirement. He doesn't want to have anything to do with the Appeal, because it involves planning and extra work. Anything that ruffles the surface of College life is an affront. He keeps cool but is more upset by what's been going on than he would like to admit. He likes normality."

"Don't we all?" Barnaby eased himself into a new position and managed to straighten one of his legs for the first time. "Brereton?"

"Can't stop coughing, poor man. Part nervous and part physical, I shouldn't wonder. A brilliant mind, I'm told. Doesn't suffer fools gladly. He's the only one I've heard criticise Duncan-Smith. Said he ought to have retired years ago—in fact, he always says what he thinks, however unpopular it may be. Something's on his mind, though. It could be the letter, it could be something else. I've spoken to him several times and every now and then it's like talking to a man who's not there."

"My impression, too."

"He can't stand the Dean, incidentally—that's Cowper. Have you met him?" Barnaby nodded, so the Brigadier went on. "A distinct atmosphere between them at breakfast this morning. Cowper didn't stop smiling in that vague way of his. It's a silly thing to say, but he looks just as he does on television. His public image seems to have taken him over."

"I haven't found his real personality yet. But I distrust men who smile too much."

Sparshott-Heyhoe grunted. "I don't like smilers."

"Intuition rather than evidence, Brigadier. But I think Cowper may have something to hide. He's clever but lacks real character—a cardboard man."

"Perhaps that's what television does for you. Never been on it myself. Don't give it house room, y'know."

"Cranston?"

"Remote—unhappy. No real friends. Respected as a scholar, particularly by Brereton. It's difficult to see him tied up with any of this. He's the sort of chap I've never really understood, so I don't think my opinion is worth much. Writes books, I'm told. Worked on the codes at Bletchley during the war—Intelligence. But I don't even know what he's a professor of. I can't see Wolfe involved either. He's the American—all gush and go. Met him? No? You haven't missed much, though he's supposed to be clever. His main concern is not to be suspected of stealing the letter."

"Any others?"

"I saw most of them yesterday evening, but only met some individually. Most live out of the College and one or two only come in occasionally. A man called Brownrigg hasn't been seen for two years and someone said he'd been eaten by cannibals in New Guinea. I think that was meant to be a joke, but you can never be quite sure with these people. There's only one other comment I feel qualified to make and that's about Luffman. You've met him?"

"Briefly, but long enough to get an impression. I like him."

"So do I. Thoroughly straightforward chap—and good with the troops from all I've seen. He's a dedicated man—and he needs to be these days. Not a port-and-pheasant priest like some of the padres I've known. No—but I've had a lot to do with men in my time and if I was responsible for Luffman I should be worried. I sat opposite him at dinner last night and I've never seen anyone so much on edge. Perfectly civil, of course, but I watched his hands and his eyes. Always watch the hands and the eyes, Inspector. Anyone told you that? Well, Luffman's near breaking point or I'm a Dutchman. The last man I saw like that shot himself in a wood near Paderborn. He'd just made off with the mess funds, y'know."

Barnaby found himself mesmerised by the staccato delivery. "Interesting. Thank you for that one. But I must get hold of Ashe first. He seems to have vanished."

"I'm not surprised. From all I've heard he's the most unpopular man in Oxford."

"That's all most helpful, Brigadier." Barnaby eased himself out of his niche and stood up. "I'm sure I can rely on you to pass on anything else you pick up. I'll do my best to clear this up as soon as possible and keep the harm done to the Appeal to the minimum. Now I really must try to find Ashe."

Barnaby's intention, from the point of view of criminal detection, was entirely sound. Unfortunately, he was to be thwarted in a way he had not foreseen: by the ill-fated luncheon of Sid Wellbeloved.

Sidney Wellbeloved would not have described himself as a gourmet; indeed, it is doubtful whether he knew the word. But he did enjoy eating his lunch in peace, and since the beginning of his feud with Ferguson this had not been possible.

The two men were porters at Oxford Station, and for the past week the mere appearance of Sidney had been sufficient to unleash a flood of invective from Ferguson. The roots of the conflict were obscure, but it had resolved itself into a struggle for control of the Down platform. Originally it had been Sid's preserve, but Ferguson, a relative newcomer, had not been slow to realise that tips on the Down were marginally higher than on the Up; accordingly, he had launched a campaign to take it over. Eventually, while Sid was away ill, Ferguson got his way, and when Sid returned to duty he refused to hand it back. Sid, a man of modest size and mild disposition, made a protest, and from then on Ferguson poured out Celtic imprecations every time they met. Normally this did not worry Sid unduly, for with Ferguson on the Down and himself on the Up their paths rarely crossed. But they did share the same lunch hour and after a week of abuse, delivered in a vocabulary with notable limitations, Sid decided to take his lunch off to a quiet corner to enjoy it in peace. As he put it afterwards, "You can take a lot, mate, but no one's goin' to put up with 'avin 'is dinner mucked about."

When the magic hour came, therefore, instead of going to the porters' restroom, where Ferguson would be lying in wait for him, he went to the freight office, where he confidently anticipated a quiet word with the clerk and an uninterrupted lunch. When he got there the clerk wasn't at his desk; indeed, the shed was deserted. He was not sorry. If he sat at the front with the clerk he would be noticed by the Station Manager, who would certainly expect him back on the platform before the 2:15 pulled out for London. On the other hand, if he tucked himself away behind the miscellaneous array of crates, parcels, and boxes, he might well let his lunch hour run on until the 2:45. With such unworthy but understandable thoughts, Sid went to the back of the shed, where sliding doors opened onto a loading ramp from the road. Here he sat down on a convenient box and put his lunch tin on a crate, which made a suitable table. From his pocket he drew two cans of beer, which he set down methodically beside the tin. The best moment of the working day had come and he anticipated with relish the lunch his wife had prepared.

She had not disappointed him. Opening the tin he found two sizable pork pies, three packets of crisps, his favourite sandwiches of cheese and pickle, some homemade apple tart, and a generous slice of ginger cake. Dieticians might have found fault with this repast, but Sid did not. He stretched for the first pork pie and his mouth watered.

The anticipation was not to be fulfilled. As he stretched, he realised his table was not standing foursquare and the beer wobbled on top of it. He looked at the base of the crate, saw it was standing unevenly on some copper pipes, and moved it to firmer ground. When he did so, the lid moved and he was aware that the crate had not been sealed. Briefly, curiosity got the better of his hunger. Steadying his beer with one hand, he slid the lid to one side with the other and peered in.

Looking up at him was the contorted face of a man who was plainly dead. The eyes bulged from their sockets; the tongue, purple and huge, protruded grotesquely; there was blood around the ears and foam beneath the nose; the skin was blotched and blue.

For an instant Sidney Wellbeloved registered this macabre vision. Then he ran out onto the platform and vomited copiously on Ferguson's Down line.

❧

The discovery of Ashe's body, unexpected though it was, did not throw Barnaby off balance as his junior colleagues had anticipated. "At least we've got some motives for this one," he grunted.

He was walking with Arnold in the cloister of Fletcher Quad, taking one gargantuan stride to his partner's two.

"Why the station, sir?"

"Can't imagine. But it doesn't look as though he was killed there. The first report says he'd been dead more than a dozen hours, possibly more. He may have been dumped."

"I can't see where he fits in with Duncan-Smith."

"Nor can I, on the face of it. But the library may be common ground. Don't forget the peace badge, and it looks as though the manuscript business may come home to roost with him."

They reached the end of the cloister by the war memorial, where oily streaks were the only reminder of the paint outrage. As they turned the corner, they almost bumped into the Dean hurrying in the opposite direction.

Cowper's smile and apology were instantaneous. "Not looking where I was going." He ran a hand through his hair in the gesture well known to television audiences. "As a matter of fact, I hoped I might see you, Inspector. I think I've been withholding information." Again the ready smile and the suggestion of a friendly confidence to come. They turned the angle of the cloister and he fell into step.

"Not intentional concealment, I hope," said Barnaby stiffly. He found Cowper's overt friendliness more difficult to deal with than the suspicion he usually met.

"No, just something that slipped my mind. Sergeant Arnold, you may remember you asked me who was in the library when I left last night. I said I didn't know. The lights were on in several of the bays, but I couldn't be certain who was there. I had the impression I'd seen Ashe come in—and Mrs. Jarvis was there, of course. That's correct. But now I remember that as I came out I passed Brereton going in. He's always in and out as librarian and it was so normal I forgot to mention it. Then it occurred to me that I ought to say I'd seen him as he would certainly mention seeing *me*. It would look odd if our stories didn't match."

"Quite right, Mr. Cowper, quite right. Yes, he did remember seeing you. The trouble is that although he went into the library he isn't sure who was working there either. He wasn't even sure of the time he arrived. Can you do any better?"

"It must have been around ten o'clock, but I could be a quarter of an hour out either way. Look here, Inspector, will it look bad for Ashe if he *was* in the library with Duncan-Smith?"

Barnaby looked at him carefully; Arnold studied his feet.

"It already looks bad for Ashe, Mr. Cowper. He was found down at the railway station this afternoon. He'd been strangled."

CHAPTER 13

THE late afternoon sun etched the pattern
of the beech tree in the Master's garden on the
pale green Wilton of his drawing-room.

"At the station?"

"Strangled with a tie." Barnaby was once more sitting in
an armchair beneath the portrait of a severe and much be-
wigged Fellow.

The Master seemed as unperturbed as ever at the news of a
further catastrophe for the institution over which he presided. Puzzlement was more apparent than shock. "Why on
earth the station?"

"Difficult to say, sir. It may be that the murderer simply
wanted to delay discovery. After all, it's difficult to know what
to do with a body. And it probably wouldn't have been found
yet if it hadn't been for this man Wellbeloved."

"It occurs to you, Inspector, that there will be no shortage
of motives in Ashe's case?"

"There are so many ends sticking out it's difficult to know
which one to pull. But I'm going to make a start with something Professor Cranston said. Can you tell me anything, sir,
about two undergraduates called Burgess and Rigby?"

Braine stood up and turned towards the window. A full
thirty seconds went by before he spoke again. When he did

so, there was an edge to his voice Barnaby had not heard before.

"I know nothing of Burgess. He had a normal career here, so far as I am aware. I believe he took a Second in Greats. Rigby is a different matter. He was a very bright boy who had a research Fellowship. Everyone predicted a great future for him, but he took to drugs, had his Fellowship withdrawn, and died soon afterwards."

"Cranston blamed Ashe."

"A lot of people did, particularly the senior Fellows. Cowper felt strongly too, because they'd done some work together." Braine crossed to a bookcase by the fireplace. "Ever heard of the Wansdyke?"

"No."

"I don't suppose many people have. It's an old earthwork running across Somerset and Wiltshire—a ditch and a bank. It's always proved something of a problem to archaeologists." He took out a slim green volume and opened it at the title page. He read aloud: *"Proceedings of the Wessex Archaeological Society."* He handed the book to Barnaby and said, "Look at the first paper in 1966."

Barnaby turned the page and read to himself: *"Romano-British Enigma: The Wansdyke Reconsidered."* Aloud he said, "By Julian Cowper, Fellow of Beaufort College, Oxford."

"If you look at the footnotes, you'll see that Cowper acknowledges a lot of help from Rigby. They worked on the dyke together, though Cowper wrote the article. It's a controversial piece of work and caused a stir when it was published. It split the archaeologists right down the middle. Everyone in the College knows about it. There's nothing like a *cause célèbre* in one discipline to attract the attention of the others."

"Ashe had nothing to do with archaeology?"

"Not as far as I know. And don't misunderstand me, Inspector. I'm not pointing a finger of suspicion at Cowper. But you asked about Rigby and he worked more closely with him than anyone else. In fact, one could say that his reputation as a scholar was made by that article."

"No, sir, I won't misinterpret you. Tell me more about Mr. Cowper."

"He's not popular. Some envy his television success, others despise it. Brereton blames him for the lack of discipline in the College, Luffman thinks he ought to go to chapel. For one who has gained so much popularity in public, he is exceedingly unsuccessful in private. But he's a notable academic. Don't dismiss him as a glib TV don who doesn't know what a real university looks like. Half the trouble with the Wansdyke business is that he's probably right. That's unforgivable in the eyes of a scholar committed to a contrary view. Perhaps we all forgive failure more easily than success." He smiled. "But I don't think he killed Ashe."

Braine looked out of the window. The sun was failing now and a fine mist was rising above the scattered beech leaves. He half shrugged his shoulders as though the ways of the world in general, and his colleagues in particular, were a mystery he no longer bothered with. "I'm sorry about Ashe. He was a tiresome person and I won't conceal the fact that life will be smoother without him. But the thought of his death is not a pleasant one."

The Master looked at his watch. "It's not too early for a sherry, I think, Inspector. I can recommend this Manzanilla—dry, but with a little body to it."

❦

Barnaby accepted the Master's sherry but declined an invitation to dine in Hall and shortly afterwards left to find Arnold, whom he had previously sent off to see how investigations into the domestic side of the College were going. The small lecture room where Sparshott-Heyhoe had talked about the Appeal had been handed over to the police, and there

94

Arnold was checking reports from two young constables.

"Nothing much here, sir," said Arnold. "With the exception of the butler, Wilson, and the porter who is on duty at night, the whole College staff live out and none of them was on hand later than ten yesterday. Once dinner has finished, the kitchen staff clear off as fast as they can. Apparently they only stay late for special dinners, gaudies, and so on. The scouts take it in turns to serve dinner, and the ten who were on duty last night had all gone home by nine forty-five. The night porter, a man called Jephson, is certain they'd all gone. He took over at eight and was in the lodge all night."

"And Wilson?"

"He served coffee in the Senior Common Room and went to his own room at about ten-fifteen. He noticed nothing in particular and went nowhere near the library. He has two rooms at the top of Lancaster Hall. But he is some use because he remembers who had left the Common Room before he went off duty himself. Apparently a number were still there, drinking port or whatever one does on these occasions, mostly Fellows who don't dine in College very often and wanted to make the most of it. These had all gone—Duncan-Smith, Luffman, Wolfe, Gibbs, Cowper, Brereton, and Plummer. And he remembers seeing the Bursar and Brigadier Sparshott-Heyhoe leaving down the main stairs just as he was going up his own side stairs to Lancaster Hall. Ashe went straight from the table—he never appeared in the Common Room for drinks after dinner at all."

"It doesn't tell us much. The man we're after could have left later than Wilson and still had time to kill Duncan-Smith before he was found at eleven. Besides, we've got two bodies now. Somehow we've got to find out Ashe's movements, both alive and dead. Anything else from the night porter? He was in a good position to see comings and goings."

"Yes, there is. He wanted to be discreet and hoped it would go no further."

"Well?"

"Apparently a young lady left the College this morning. He's certain she didn't come in through the main gate today, so he assumes she was in the College all night. He happens to know her name is Miss Ferrers, and she's currently going around with Ashe and Plummer. Staff gossip has it that she's just thrown Ashe out of her flat in Holywell and has taken up with Plummer."

"Any idea why she went out of the main gate when she hadn't come in that way?"

"He assumed she'd been let into the College the night before, probably by Plummer. He'd have a key to the postern."

"Why didn't she go out that way?"

"Probably because we had a man on that gate after the discovery of the old man's body."

"I see. Yes, well that ties up with what Plummer told me. I think we can be discreet, but we'll have to see her. Anything else?"

"Only a small thing, sir, and probably worth nothing. There's been a fuller report about Ashe. Apparently he was strangled with a tie, a Beaufort College tie."

Barnaby's eyebrows arched, dominating the prominent bone structure of his face. "His own?"

"No. I'm told he never wore a College tie—it was all part of his protest. No, the interesting thing is that it was a brand-new tie. It had never been tied, as a tie, at all."

"Certainly odd. Check the make of tie, and we'll find the shop that sold it."

"I've started on that. It's pure silk and that narrows the field. Most College ties are Terylene these days." Arnold coughed. "There is one other small point, though I don't suppose it's important."

"Yes?"

"Jephson tells me there is one don who always wears a Beaufort tie. It's almost a College joke."

"Who's that?"

"The Master—Sir Michael Braine."

"Braine?" Barnaby ran his hand over his hair in a gesture unconsciously copied from Cowper. Was it possible that his quarry had a gruesome sense of humour?

CHAPTER 14

AT seven o'clock Barnaby retired to the Eastgate Hotel for a snack, leaving Arnold on duty in Beaufort. After rushing about all day, he wanted to detach himself from the atmosphere in the College to mull over the material he had so far. He collected a pint of beer and some sandwiches and retreated to a corner of the lounge. He took out a notebook and made occasional jottings.

On the face of it he was dealing with a series of crimes that might or might not be related. The theft and subsequent destruction of the manuscript, as well as the daubing of the war memorial, could be considered as disconnected items of vandalism or a prologue to the ensuing tragedy. Several circumstances linked them tenuously with the murders. First, Plummer—assuming he was telling the truth—suspected Ashe of the paint daubing and, secondly, the seal found in Ashe's room had been confirmed as the seal from the letter. Furthermore, if Cowper was to be believed, Ashe had been in the library shortly before Duncan-Smith's death. Then Ashe was the final victim, or at least the final discovery. The common factor throughout was Ashe.

Motives for the murder of the old man appeared to be nonexistent, but for Ashe they were legion; or if that was too strong, he had yet to meet one person who had a good word to say for him. Perhaps the motive was not the best way of going about it. If there was a weak point in the murderer's defence, it was likely to be in Ashe's transportation to the station. Had he been alive? The first estimate of time of death suggested he had died at approximately the same time as Duncan-Smith, and, if that was right, intuition told him he had probably travelled as a corpse. How had he left the College? The porter had not seen him go out of the main gate, so it must have been the postern. If he'd gone out alive, he could have used his own key. On the other hand, if he had gone out dead he would have been carried. Who was strong enough to carry a body by himself? Of the Fellows only Luffman and Plummer looked like possibilities, but desperation can give strength . . .

Somewhere a car must come into it. Ashe must have been driven, alive or dead. That meant the chance that the car had been noticed, particularly if Ashe had been carried as a corpse either at the beginning or end of the journey. So cars must be checked; as yet he had no idea who had cars and who did not.

It was difficult to hazard a hypothesis for events in the library. Had Ashe for some reason murdered Duncan-Smith and then been killed by a third party arriving inopportunely? Might Ashe and a third person have killed Duncan-Smith jointly and then fallen out among themselves? Or was it conceivable that the old man had plotted with someone to kill Ashe but had himself been killed during the execution of the plan? Or could it be that an unknown third person had killed both Ashe and Duncan-Smith and for some reason moved only one of the bodies? If that was the case, he had to add, why had the murderer strangled one and killed the other with a blow or blows?

The discovery of Ashe's peace badge certainly suggested he had been in the library at the critical time and in the bay next to the Professor, though it could, of course, be a plant. But why were the books in that bay out of order? Perhaps

99

something had been hidden behind them and they had been put back in a hurry. What could have been hidden? A weapon to hit Duncan-Smith with? If so, where was it? Hardly the tie. The killer could have brought that in his pocket. And somewhere in the centre of it all was the Beaufort manuscript; he was beginning to cling onto that as an article of faith.

Barnaby chewed a chicken sandwich with care, reflecting on the myriad possibilities. The tie suggested premeditation. Had it been round someone's neck, actually being used as a tie, it might have been spontaneous; but as it was brand-new and had never been used, the suspicion was that it had been bought for the special purpose. In that case the murder of Ashe might be premeditated, while that of the old man was not. That was better—unless, of course, there was a weapon yet to be found.

Then there was the whole question of who had been in the region of the library at the critical time. Apart from Ashe and the old man, there were no certainties. He planned to see Mrs. Jarvis in a few minutes, but she would only cover the time to the closing of the library. Any Fellow could have entered with his own key afterwards and no one any the wiser. Only by a process of alibi investigation and elimination could that one be dealt with, a routine piece of spade-work.

He thought again of Ashe, the College rebel. What about the vandalism for which he was being blamed? Was it all too easy? Blame Ashe—and now he was dead. He felt the letter was the starting point for the case, and he was aware of a nagging doubt about it. Something didn't fit, something he ought to see very clearly if only he could look at it from the right angle.

Too much speculation and not enough hard fact. But one fact stood out. Plummer obviously disliked Ashe. It wasn't what he had said about him, but the way he had said it. He'd only been with the man a few minutes and Ashe had been peripheral to their conversation, but the bitterness stood out a mile. If that was so, could Plummer be trusted when he identified Ashe as the paint vandal? Speculation again.

He looked at his watch. Yes, it was time to see Mrs. Jarvis. He drained his beer and hoisted himself upright, his body moving in its disjointed way. Outside, the autumnal mist was turning into an October fog. Cars in the High had headlamps on as they curved up past St. Mary's or down to Magdalen Bridge; the traffic lights at the junction with Longwall Street glowed dully.

Barnaby was just turning away from the High towards Beaufort when a lean shape, walking briskly, emerged from the fog. It was Brereton, his face somehow thinner and more ascetic in the gloom. He recognised Barnaby and stopped in front of him.

"Good evening, Inspector. A happy meeting—I have something to tell you and it's less embarrassing than seeing you in College."

"Good evening, Mr. Brereton. Do you want to talk here or go somewhere quieter?"

"Let's take a turn up the High. It won't take long, but I'd rather we weren't overheard."

They went past the Divinity Schools, both men adapting their normally brisk pace to the conspiratorial tone of their conversation.

"I understand, Inspector, that Ashe has been found in—ah —awkward circumstances."

"You could put it that way, sir."

"You'll find plenty of people glad to see the back of Ashe."

Barnaby eyed Brereton obliquely. Did he detect a certain unease in that bland statement? "Yes, I've gathered that."

"Has anyone mentioned the name . . ." Brereton paused as though it was difficult to pronounce. "The name of Rigby?"

"It has been mentioned."

"Do you know what happened to him?"

"Tell me, sir."

101

"He was an undergraduate at Beaufort and later a research Fellow. He lost his Fellowship, joined a left-wing commune, and died a heroin addict."

Barnaby was aware of more than unease now. There was a tension in Brereton's voice he had not heard before, and his words came tumbling out.

"Ashe was the main influence on Rigby at a critical time. He warped his ideals."

"Can you think of anyone who would murder him?"

"Murder is not easy, Inspector—at least I would not find it so. But most of us disliked Ashe. Luffman couldn't stand his attitude to the chapel, Rigby was Cowper's pupil and colleague when they worked on the Wansdyke, the Master didn't see how to get rid of him legally, Cranston . . . The list is endless. You'll find bitterness everywhere."

"Was Cowper upset?"

"We were all upset—there was a lot of feeling in the College. Several of us wanted Ashe deprived of his Fellowship, but the Master didn't want a scandal."

They reached Magpie Lane and by common consent turned down towards Beaufort.

"Could Ashe have destroyed the letter—in your opinion, sir?"

"A naïve question, if you don't mind my saying so, Inspector. Ashe was not bound by the conventions of society. He despised them. Yes, he could have destroyed the letter—very easily. I even wonder if he could have gone as far as killing Duncan-Smith. Have you considered that?"

"We're trying to consider everything. There could be a hundred and one motives we haven't discovered yet. I must ask you one question, Mr. Brereton. That list of names you said was endless just now, of those who disliked Ashe. Would your name be on that list, sir?"

Brereton's incisive features turned towards Barnaby, his eyes glinting in the light of a lamp hanging from the College wall.

"Most certainly, Inspector, most certainly."

He turned away and let himself through the postern gate. Barnaby heard his cough echo in the cloisters.

Back in the College, Barnaby made his way to the library. The fog, thicker now, deadened the noise of traffic from outside, and the sound of his footsteps on the flagstones reverberated ahead of him. Across Fletcher Quad the lights from the library cast an opalescent glow, suggesting remote warmth. The College clock struck the half hour, its notes muffled in the night.

Mrs. Jarvis was sitting at her desk, which lay back in the first bay. She was small, bespectacled, tight-lipped, with a brittle smile. Barnaby reached her desk in two enormous strides and introduced himself. "Are we alone?" he asked.

"Yes. When I arrived there was a constable here, poking about in the bays at the end, but he went about half an hour ago. We haven't been letting undergraduates in. If they want a book I get it for them."

Barnaby picked up a chair and sat down. "Now, Mrs. Jarvis," he began, thrusting his head forward, "I want to clear up some details about last night. So far everybody has been very vague about who was here and who wasn't."

Mrs. Jarvis patted the bun at the back of her head. "I'll do my best, Inspector."

"What time did you leave the library?"

"I locked up at the usual time—ten o'clock. I suppose I left a minute or two after."

"Who was still here?"

"All the undergraduates had gone—they're not allowed in after ten. Shortly before I locked up, the Dean left and at just about the same time Mr. Brereton came in. When I left, he was working at some papers at his desk over there. There were two other Fellows in here working—Mr. Duncan-Smith and"—her voice was coloured by a new quality—"and Mr. Ashe."

"Where were they sitting?"

"Mr. Duncan-Smith was in the bay where he was found and Mr. Ashe was in the bay next door. There is just one thing I should mention. Earlier on, the American—Mr. Wolfe—came into the library, but I didn't see him leave. I've been thinking about it, of course, since I heard of the poor old man's death and I really can't be sure whether he was in the library or not. He certainly wasn't in the main hall up here—I would have seen him as I moved about—but he might have been down in the basement. On the other hand, I don't check people in and out, and he could easily have slipped out when I wasn't looking."

"I see—well, I'll speak to him. Now can you tell me about the books in that bay? Sergeant Arnold tells me some of them were out of order, the Pitt speeches and so on."

"Yes, Sergeant Arnold mentioned them to me. I'm quite sure they were all right at about six that evening. You see, I collected one or two books from that bay to go away for rebinding and I checked the shelves automatically."

"You're certain?"

"Positive. Librarians have an eye for that sort of thing. Psychologists have a rude word for it, I believe. It was the same with the box."

"What box?"

"A crate really, not a box, Inspector. For the books needing rebinding. We send a large consignment once a year. Some—the ordinary books—go up to Scotland and the older leatherbound ones go to a specialist in London."

"What's wrong with the box?"

"It's missing." The statement was simple and spoken ingenuously; Barnaby allowed his eyes to narrow fractionally. "Yes," she continued, "there were three and now there are two."

She explained as though to a child. "Let me show you."

She led the way to an unlighted area behind the catalogue where two large crates stood in the shadows. They were as tall as tea chests and substantially broader; each had *Beaufort College Library* stencilled on the side.

Barnaby tapped the nearest one. "Empty?"

"Yes. We collect the books together first and list them before packing them up."

"When did you notice one was missing?"

"Soon after I came in this evening. I've looked everywhere, including the stack-room downstairs. It's gone."

"I know where it is, Mrs. Jarvis."

She looked at him blankly.

"It's down at the station with Mr. Ashe's body in it."

Mrs. Jarvis stared at him, then turned away. "The whole business is making me sick, physically sick. I can't stand David Ashe, but this is . . . awful." She seemed impressed by the inadequacy of the word. "Disgusting. Everything's been wrong in the College since the manuscript was stolen. That was the start of it, I'm sure."

"The letter came back this morning. It's been torn up and is quite beyond repair."

The light glinted on Mrs. Jarvis's glasses. She searched vainly for words and seemed about to burst into tears.

As Barnaby watched her, a thought in the recesses of his mind suddenly moved into focus. He excused himself hurriedly and went out into the cloister.

The fog, thicker now, drifted beneath the arches of the cloister. A group of undergraduates, mere shapes ahead of him, made their way from the Buttery to the Junior Common Room. From the chapel, quite invisible across the quad, came the strains of the organ.

The point that had occurred to Barnaby was a simple one. Until this moment he had assumed Ashe to have been responsible for the destruction of the manuscript and for sending it to the Bursar. But the envelope containing the remains had been inserted into the *second post*. While it might have been possible for someone in the College to have left an internal letter the previous night for delivery with the first post, if it was to arrive by the second it would have to be slipped in during the morning. So whoever sent it to the Bursar, it could not have been Ashe. For by the morning Ashe was already dead.

Later, as Barnaby undressed in the small guest room perched high in Beauchamp Quad, he found himself thinking along lines rather different from those he had followed earlier in the Eastgate.

In the first place there was the manuscript. Whether he admitted it or not, he had been working on the assumption that Ashe had stolen it, destroyed it and, for some reason, sent the remains to the Bursar. Now he had to face the fact that someone else had sent it. Ergo, either someone knew Ashe had it and sent it after his death, or Ashe had never been connected with it at all and the seal was merely a plant to set him up for the police. Both alternatives were awkward and destroyed preconceived theories.

Then there was this constant talk of Rigby. His death was clearly blamed on Ashe, and although it had taken place several years ago it was remarkably fresh in the consciousness of the College. Cranston, Braine, Luffman, Brereton—they'd all mentioned it, and as far as he could see it was independent comment. No link with Duncan-Smith, of course . . .

Barnaby hung his trousers methodically on a flimsy wire hanger and put them in the wardrobe. He put on his green striped pyjamas and shivered as he looked out into the fog.

The central heating was only a modest success, and he climbed into bed with a sense of relief.

How far was the letter part of the affair anyway? It could hardly be related to Duncan-Smith by anything he knew so far. But nothing related to him. His death was the one fact that refused to fit into any context he could devise. It was so out of place it looked almost like a chance happening.

A chance happening? The thought was sudden and somehow shocking. Could it be that the death that had transformed vandalism into murder was in some way irrelevant to the whole affair, a red herring obscuring the logic of other events? Suppose Duncan-Smith had been killed by accident. Had he, perhaps, tried to stop Ashe from perpetrating another piece of wanton damage? Might he have been killed in mistake for Ashe? Hardly. The physical contrast between the old man and the young was too great. From behind? No, he could not have been approached from behind in the reading bay.

Barnaby stretched out a hand and turned off the lamp on the bedside table. The room was suddenly dark, the only light the soft glow of a gas lamp in Magpie Lane. Darkness. Suppose the library had been in darkness. But the light had been on in the bay when Duncan-Smith was found. Yes, but suppose it had been out at the time of the murder. The thought that he might have been killed by mistake appealed to Barnaby, if only because it covered the complete lack of motive for his death.

Where did Plummer and his girl friend fit in—if at all? To begin with, he had been inclined to discount them, and he had been impressed by Plummer's apparent frankness. But Ashe's death had altered things. He had not failed to notice the porter's hint of an irregular triangle of which Ashe formed a part, and it need not be coincidence that Ferrers had been in the College at the critical time. And Plummer had clearly shown dislike of Ashe. A mere rival, or something else?

Barnaby stretched his legs and found, as usual, that he was too long for the bed. "Built for a dwarf," he muttered.

Even as he spoke, he had a vision of the laundryman carrying the laundry basket across the quad and out of the College. "I wonder . . ." And he had another vision of a corpse being carried out of the postern gate in a crate labelled *Beaufort College Library*.

❧

By midmorning the following day some questions were acquiring answers. The ownership of cars had been easily dealt with. Of the Fellows in College on the night of the murder only Ashe did not own a car. The rest had vehicles that did much to justify the theory that a car is an extension of the personality. Plummer had a two-seat Morgan, green, rather faded, and very English; he drove it open on all occasions. The Master had a prewar Lagonda, a car of character and distinction, maintained with loving care and at low cost by Wilson, whose engineering knowledge was used at all mechanical points of the College. By contrast, Wolfe had hired an orange Volkswagen for the duration of his stay, and Cranston had a family saloon, a Vauxhall. Brereton drove a mature Morris Traveller, Farquhar a large Ford Estate, usually full of his numerous progeny, and Cowper a white Volvo, which he felt enhanced his status as don-about-town. Luffman ran a very rusty Hillman Minx, and Duncan-Smith owned a Wolseley, which was untaxed and had been off the road for two years, since its driver had knocked down a keep-left sign in Slough.

On two fronts, reports were totally negative. There were no prints on the remains of the manuscript or on the envelope. No one at the porter's lodge recalled anyone's interfering with the second post, and it had not yet been possible to trace the machine that had typed the address. Likewise, in spite of considerable research at Oxford tailors, none would admit selling the Beaufort tie; indeed, none admitted stocking ties of this particular quality, and one or two said it was a type that had gone out of production several years ago.

Barnaby gathered this information from Arnold in the lecture room, then went to call on Caroline Ferrers in Holywell. The overnight fog had cleared, leaving a heavy, damp atmosphere. The clouds were low and a mild wind from the west threatened rain. When he got no answer to his ringing, he realised she was out and his walk seemed wasted. He looked morosely into a window full of musical scores, avoided a bicycle being pushed out of an alley by a hirsute undergraduate, and made his way to the Broad, where a late-season American package tour debouched, cameras dangling, from the Sheldonian. Grunting to himself and lengthening his stride, Barnaby turned down the Turl to avoid them, then into Queen's Lane, tracing his way back to Beaufort between the walls of New College and Queen's.

At the back of Queen's, parked in a narrow space by the Provost's Lodging, stood a large green car of uncertain vintage. The near-side door opened as Barnaby walked past and Sir Michael Braine's carefully groomed head appeared, his features looking more concerned than at any previous stage in the enquiry.

"Hullo, Barnaby. I'm glad I've caught you. Let me give you a lift back to Beaufort. It'll take longer than walking with this confounded traffic, but I'd appreciate a word with you."

Barnaby climbed aboard the Lagonda as though getting into a carriage. The Master did not start the engine at once but sat staring over the steering wheel. At length he said, "I've just been to see the Provost. He's an old friend of mine."

Barnaby did not think this needed a response, so he fixed his eye on the tower of St. Peter's Church rising next to St. Edmund Hall, and remained silent. Somewhere near at hand a clock chimed the hour, to be followed at intervals by others.

"I've been asking his advice about our problems at Beau-

110

fort. You see, Inspector, I have to tell you something—something about which I have been rather less than honest."

"Yes, sir?"

"On the night Duncan-Smith was killed, Professor Cranston came to see me quite late. We both told you that, and I believe he told you why he came. Two things I did not tell you. First, there was the state he was in. The moment I saw him at the door, I knew something was wrong. He was grey—a greyness I have only seen previously in men suffering a terminal illness. I asked him what was the matter and he explained about the telephone call from Ashe—as he believed it to be. But that had taken place earlier in the day and he looked perfectly all right at dinner. He had a whisky, we talked for a while, and by the time he left he was much more his usual self. It was then, just as he was leaving, that I noticed the second thing. The sleeve of his jacket was torn, and there was a fresh scratch on the side of his hand."

Braine stopped abruptly, glanced at Barnaby, and then held up his hand. "Now before you expostulate, Inspector, you must see this from my point of view. I believed his story of the telephone call and I was touched that a man of his distinction should confide in me. Frankly I could not—and cannot—believe he is implicated in this business. Moreover, I felt almost like a priest in the confessional, and even now I'm not sure I'm doing the right thing. In a way he bared his soul—he even told me about his feelings for that boy from Magdalen. Besides, Cranston is a man of probity and reputation. Nevertheless, I have come to the conclusion that I am wrong to withhold anything that may be relevant."

Barnaby controlled the feelings that first sprang to the surface. He said simply, "You say his sleeve was torn?"

"Yes. It was the sort of tear anyone might get, but I noticed it because Cranston is meticulous in his dress and it happened to be just above the scratch on his hand. It was as though both had been caught at the same time—on a nail, perhaps."

111

Braine reverted to his normal relaxed style now that he had imparted his information. He started the engine and pulled out into Queen's Lane. The size of the car emphasised his own small stature as he struggled with the steering wheel. It seemed unlikely he could see much beyond the bonnet, and the car swung hazardously like an unresponsive ship in a heavy swell. "It's going to rain, I think," he observed blandly.

∾

Quentin Luffman sat at his desk and stared out at the low clouds over Fletcher Quad; a piece of fair hair fell over his right eye, making him look younger than usual. At Sparshott-Heyhoe's behest, he was working on a draft for the Appeal, a blurb on the beauties of the chapel and the need for restoration, to be incorporated in the brochure along with the other College derelictions.

Beaufort Chapel is unique in Oxford, he had written, truthfully but without inspiration. *Conceived by an unknown medieval artist and executed by craftsmen whose meticulous attention to detail we, in an age of mass production, cannot begin to understand, the chapel has been added to by succeeding generations until it is now a microcosm of the history of the College.*

"Pretty trite," he thought. He really ought to say it's now a bastard hotchpotch, neither one thing nor the other, a medieval gem corrupted by the arrogance of posterity. He looked across the quad to the high perpendicular windows, contrasting their clean lines with the ornate and ill-conceived detail of the entrance porch where the Victorians had done their worst.

The first spots of windblown rain marked his window. A knock came at the door.

"Come in."

It was Malcolm Broadhead, still fingering his embryonic beard; it did not seem to have made much progress, Luffman observed. At the same time he had a sense of *déjà vu* as the

112

stocky boy sat down opposite him, looking nervously at his feet.

"I suppose you wonder why I've come."

"I imagine it's connected with our conversation of the other day."

"Things have changed."

"You mean Ashe is dead."

"Yes, Mr. Luffman, Ashe is dead."

Luffman felt strangely guilty under Broadhead's careful brown eyes. "It doesn't alter what I said about him."

"It's not his death I've come about. It's the letter."

"You know who had it?"

"Yes."

"You would rather tell me than the police?" He was trying to rebuild the frail relationship they had once had.

"I don't like the bloody police." The expletive fell unnaturally from his lips.

"You have to work hard to be a rebel, don't you?"

"My bourgeois upbringing. Ashe had the letter. I saw it in his room. He showed it to me."

"Were you the only one?"

"As far as I know."

"What was he going to do with it?"

"Exactly what he did. Destroy it—as he wanted to destroy the College and everything it stands for."

"Did you see him do it?"

"No. He said he was reserving it for someone. I got the impression he was going to make a ceremony of it in front of one of the College bigwigs. I thought it might be the Master."

"You know the letter *was* destroyed and sent to the Bursar?"

"It's common knowledge in the Junior Common Room. He must have done it before he was killed. That's why I've come to see you."

"None of the Fellows knew what had happened to it until

113

the Bursar received the remains, and that was after Ashe was dead."

"How do you know that?" asked Broadhead, looking out of the window where the rain was now streaming down. "I know what he intended to do, and I believe he was killed for it."

Luffman pushed the papers on his desk away from him. He turned to face Broadhead. "I hated Ashe. I've told you that already. I have no regrets over his death. But I'm bound to pass your information on to the police."

"Of course you are."

"And they will undoubtedly want to see you."

Broadhead stood up abruptly. "I don't care. I'll play this according to society's rules if I have to. Ashe wasn't perfect— I'm not fool enough to believe that. But he saw that Fabian reform does nothing but preserve class injustice in a disguised form. The only way is a new start, to destroy the canker of elitism that corrupts everything."

"You're making a speech, Malcolm. Let's try to keep it simple." He smiled, still trying to find common ground. "I know you're an idealist and I respect some of your principles. But Ashe was not a man of ideals. He was completely negative, completely destructive. I have never met a man for whom I have had such a detestation."

"And you a Christian, full of forgiveness?"

"I am a Christian, but my Christianity is not a sloppy creed with prizes for all." There was a new intensity in his tone. "My compassion is for those Ashe led astray—like Rigby. There is a just vengeance theologians cannot get rid of however hard they try. Ashe is dead, and he deserved to die."

There was a silence, broken only when Luffman said, "Now I'm preaching a sermon. Unless there is anything else you want to tell me, we'd better leave it at that."

Broadhead's hand returned to his beard; he blinked. He was face to face with an emotion beyond the range of his experience.

114

SPARSHOTT-HEYHOE eyed the woman his firm had sent to be his secretary with gloom. She was a spinster of indeterminate middle age, with a florid face and an immense capacity for cream pastries. He wondered how long he could put up with her and considered writing a stiff note to Personnel.

"Miss Crisp"—her name alone should have ruled her out of court—"Miss Crisp, I want to start the card index this morning. As you know, we shall want all the old Beaufort men arranged alphabetically, but the Bursar has them according to years of matriculation so we shall have to work through them. I believe he has the first batch ready, so would you please be kind enough to fetch them up."

Miss Crisp managed a sickly smile. "Yes, Brigadier. Of course." Clumsily she manoeuvred in the close confines of the office, dislodging a pile of papers from the desk as she made a final gyration at the door.

Sparshott-Heyhoe groaned inwardly as he listened to her progress down two flights of uncarpeted stairs. Then he took out some coloured index cards and began to arrange them in piles in front of him. This was a scheme of his own devising, based on certain random associations. Thus, as a cricketer, he gave old members living in Yorkshire a white card, those in

Lancashire red. Thinking vaguely of corn, he allotted East Anglia yellow, while memories of wet holidays in Cornwall gave the Southwest grey. London was blue, as there were always more blue cards than any others; Wales was green, because in a moment of aberration he had confused it with Ireland; while those living abroad had an appalling shade of purple that he felt was appropriate for those who had made such a bizarre choice of habitat.

Once on a card, complete with address and profession, each man would be given a star rating, according to his likely response to the Appeal. Three stars indicated a possible four-figure donation, one meant something decidedly less ambitious. Later, when the first phase was over, those who had failed to give at all would be identified with a black spot and earmarked for a second, more forceful approach.

By the time blundering sounds on the stairs heralded the return of Miss Crisp, the Brigadier had arranged his cards and was sticking coloured flags into the wall map over his head. She came into the room backwards, carrying four trays of index cards; her face was redder than ever and she was breathing heavily; a cobweb on her hair testified to a visit to one of the remoter fastnesses of the Bursar's office. She sneezed loudly.

"It's the dust, Brigadier."

"Yes, Miss Crisp. Now put them down over there and let's start."

"Shall we begin with the letter A, Brigadier?"

"That would be logical, Miss Crisp."

❧

Miss Crisp was not the only caller at the Bursar's office that morning. Shortly after the rain started, Sergeant Arnold arrived, following Barnaby's injunction to "Find out about Rigby." He fought his way through an array of clerks, ranging from an elderly Dickensian personage whom he naturally addressed as "sir" to a brace of vacuous secretaries giving each other a manicure. But the Bursar was himself on hand and had given instructions that any police enquiries should go directly to him. Accordingly, Arnold was shown through to an inner sanctum where Farquhar greeted him affably.

"I had a feeling you'd be poking about here soon, Sergeant. What can I do for you?"

"We're interested in a young research Fellow who was here a year or two ago, sir. I should . . ."

"Rigby?"

"Exactly."

"It had to be. I don't know that he had anything to do with Duncan-Smith, but once I heard Ashe was dead I knew you'd want to follow that one up. The Fellows all blamed Ashe for what happened. It's the only thing they've all agreed on since I've been here."

"How long is that, sir?"

"Just over twenty years. I stayed on in the RAF for several years after the war, then had a foray into business before coming to Beaufort. Since then I've just fallen into a comfortable rut. I'm not a dedicated bursar, but the admin. isn't difficult and it pays the school fees."

Farquhar, who had seemed on edge when Arnold arrived, was relaxing. He smiled, showing a set of regular teeth that fitted his trim appearance.

"What can you let me know about Rigby, sir? Presumably you have a record of everybody here?"

"Yes, we keep record cards giving the basic information on each man—educational record, home address, date of matriculation, and so on. Then there are the confidential files."

"I'd like to see both, please."

"Right. If you come next door, we'll get his card. The files are locked up downstairs. As a matter of fact, we've been getting the cards out for the Appeal."

They went into a small adjoining room full of wooden cabinets covered with dust. Farquhar pulled out a drawer of cards.

"Everybody who's ever been connected with the College has one of these—dons, undergraduates, and visiting scholars. We try to keep all the information up to date. Here's Rigby."

Arnold took the proffered card. It was strictly factual:

> RIGBY, Terence Charles (C. of E.)
> Born Barnstaple 1944—educated Blundells School—Open Scholarship in History 1961—Preliminary Examination, Honour School of Modern History 1963—First Class Honours Modern History 1965—elected to research Fellowship 1967—de Mowbray Prize 1969—Fellowship terminated by Governing Body 1972—deceased 1973
> Parents: Father deceased; Mother: Mrs M. Rigby
> Address: Yeo Cottage, Kentisbury Ford, Barnstaple, Devon

"A distinguished career cut short," commented Farquhar. "A tragedy."

"That's what everyone says."

"It's true. And Cowper, of course, lost a colleague."

"Was he a friend of yours?"

"Not particularly. I liked him—everyone did, until Ashe got hold of him—but we didn't have much to do with each other. Just occasionally we sat together at dinner. He was interested in the war and tried to get me to talk about it."

"Any particular friends, apart from Cowper and Ashe?"

"He got on well with Luffman's brother, who used to be in the College. They were leading lights in several Christian societies together until Rigby defected. Of the senior Fellows he probably got on best with Cranston. They used to play bridge together, and I know that Cranston did his best to get him off drugs near the end. He saw a good deal of Rigby's mother, who was trying to do the same thing. He went to stay with her for a time when Rigby died—when she needed a shoulder to lean on."

"Did he have anything to do with Duncan-Smith?"

"Not as far as I know. Frankly, I doubt if the old man ever knew who he was." Farquhar laughed abruptly. "It will be something of a relief not to have the old boy at meetings of the Governing Body anymore. We usually took it for granted he was asleep, then he would suddenly cut in with some devastatingly apt remark that showed he couldn't be written off yet. Then there was some fiddling admin. decision to be taken and he really *was* asleep, and we had to wake him up and go through the whole dreary business again before he could vote. Goodness knows how he got himself murdered."

"Shall we get the file now, sir?"

"Yes, of course. If you'll follow me."

They went downstairs to a storeroom containing piles of account books and a number of metal filing cabinets. Farquhar unlocked one and thumbed through the files inside. After a moment or two of searching he frowned, then opened another drawer. At length he turned to Arnold; his expression registered the concern of one to whom administrative untidiness is an affront.

"It's very odd, Sergeant. Rigby's file seems to have gone."

༄

Julian Cowper was having a trying time. Hitherto, by judicious arrangement of his lectures and tutorial programme, he had had little difficulty in combining his academic life at Oxford with the public appearances that made him known elsewhere. But now, for a number of reasons, things were getting out of hand.

In the first place he was giving a series of lectures on the pre-Conquest Church, and although he had prepared five during the summer vacation he had hoped to find time during the term to complete the last three. This he had not yet managed to do. Then the BBC had badgered him into compèring and acting as general nanny to a television series called "The March of Progress," a trite but time-consuming résumé of popular history planned to cover fifteen programmes. Transmission was meant for the following spring and the whole thing was already wildly behind schedule. Quite apart from the tedium of encapsulating history for general consumption, he was having difficulty with a producer who wanted every episode flavoured with what he called "social comment," a phrase that meant, in practice, arranging the facts in such a way as to show anyone in authority as a rogue or fool and all the rest as suffering innocents. This he justified in the interests of what he called "social responsibility," a concept which, as far as Cowper could see, had little to do with historical truth.

And now, with the College making national headlines and Fleet Street hungry for more revelations, the Master had deputed him to handle the press.

"You'll do it so well, Julian," he had said. "You're really the only one who understands the media. I just get angry, and I'm sure that's quite the wrong thing to do."

Cowper looked balefully at the handful of correspondents he had agreed to meet in the lecture room. They sat around smoking, watchful but affecting boredom.

"Gentlemen," said Cowper, "you will understand that the deaths of Professor Duncan-Smith and Mr. Ashe are being investigated by the police, so there is little I can properly tell you. However, the Master has asked me to say that in the meanwhile the College is working normally and, distressing though these events must be to an institution of the reputation of Beaufort, no useful purpose can be served by idle speculation, or indeed by investigation by anyone other than the proper authority. Accordingly, gentlemen, we should be grateful if you would respect the privacy of all members of the College, particularly the undergraduates, and address any enquiries about the case to the police."

"Aw, come off it, Mr. Cowper," said a small fleshy man, with whom the Dean had a slight acquaintance. "You're talking like a politician."

"That's why I was asked to deal with you."

"We understand, Mr. Cowper, that Ashe was a Maoist. Is that correct?"

"Mr. Ashe was primarily an outstanding mathematician

120

and that was why he was elected to his Fellowship. He had decided political views, however, and so far as I am aware he never made any attempt to hide them. Indeed, though I have not read them myself I believe they are in print in several journals."

"Was there ever any attempt to deprive Mr. Ashe of his Fellowship?"

"That is not a question I can answer. All I will say is that Beaufort Fellowships are for life and can only be terminated by a lengthy legal process. It has not happened this century and there is no reason to suppose it would have done so in Mr. Ashe's case."

"It's common knowledge that the war memorial was defaced shortly before the two murders. Does the College know who was responsible for that?"

"No. It is in the hands of the police."

"In view of recent events, Mr. Cowper, will the College be going ahead with the Appeal which, it is rumoured, is about to be launched?"

"I must sidestep that one, I'm afraid."

There was a pause while the journalists sought a question that might evade the Dean's stonewalling. Then a man with a prominent nose and insensitive eyes said, "Mr. Cowper, it has been suggested to me by a don from another College—and there are rumours in the university—that as you are well known for an article on the Wansdyke that you wrote with a young man called Rigby, you might not feel too badly about Mr. Ashe's death. Would you care to comment?"

Cowper's urbane, confident smile faded into a brittle mask.

"No," he said slowly. "I would not."

CHAPTER 17

DRIVEN back to Beaufort by the Master, Barnaby declined the inevitable sherry before lunch and escaped for more sandwiches at the Eastgate, where he had agreed to meet Arnold to catch up on the morning's work.

A little more information had been gathered, though again much of it was negative. Broadhead had made a statement, but added nothing to his interview with Luffman. All the undergraduates who had been in the library on the evening of Duncan-Smith's death had been seen, but no new information had emerged. The only small point of interest was that those who had noticed Duncan-Smith were pretty sure he was asleep—one claimed to have heard him snore—so it looked as though he was still alive when the library closed. Undergraduates whose rooms were near the library had been interviewed and a couple of constables were currently working through the rest of the College, but, again, any information merely served to confirm what was known already. Another constable had tried to see Wolfe to check whether he had left the library before Mrs. Jarvis locked up, but the American was not to be found. A message was left that the police wanted to see him. There were negative reports on the dons' cars. All had been checked, but none contained anything to link them with the transport of a body to the railway station. There was no sign of the missing Rigby file.

"The Bursar says he and the Senior Tutor are the only ones who have access to the confidential files," explained Arnold. "That is, the files of undergraduates who have left. The Senior Tutor—that's Professor Cranston—is responsible for the files of those who are still here, and he keeps them until they leave. Then he hands them over to the Bursar for storage."

"Who could have got at them in the Bursar's office?"

"Farquhar is positive nobody could have done. He says his key organisation is not the greatest security system in the world, but it's entirely private to himself, and he can't remember letting the keys out of his possession. Cranston says the same."

"If we accept that—and you seem prepared to, Sergeant—there are two possibilities." Barnaby leaned back in his chair; he was coming to terms with the case and was prepared to be didactic.

Arnold, who felt he should respond, put down his tankard and said, "One must be that it was Farquhar himself."

"Certainly. Though as yet, Sergeant"—he wagged a finger—"as yet we have nothing at all to suggest any connection between him and Rigby."

"Acting for somebody?"

"Perhaps. But that suggests a collusion rare in murder cases. No, I tend to the second conclusion."

"Which is?"

"That the file was never handed to the Bursar in the first place."

"Cranston?"

"Not necessarily. We don't even know if he *was* Senior Tutor when Rigby was here. In any case it need not have been the Senior Tutor himself. Presumably the files could have been interfered with while in his keeping and he none the wiser. I've sent a message asking Cranston and Brereton to come and have a word with us here after lunch in Hall. Apart from the Master, they're the two senior men and I want this file business clarified."

"It's amazing how well they all remember Rigby. Even Luffman, and he wasn't even here with him."

"Ah!" Barnaby waved his finger again. "There you have it. They all remember Rigby very well—perhaps too well. Suppose, Sergeant, suppose the file for Rigby *never existed*."

He smiled over the tips of his fingers, which he had joined together as if in prayer.

✦

Sparshott-Heyhoe and Miss Crisp were making slow progress. Large numbers of A's had attended Beaufort and their cards were piling up. Andersons, Andrews, Annandales, Annersleys, Ansteys—there seemed no end to them, or to Miss Crisp's trivial comments.

"Anstruther-Garnett," she said, picking up the next card. "What an extraordinary name!"

The Brigadier glowered. "Several of us have odd names, Miss Crisp. Now do let us get on."

✦

"There's not much doubt," said Barnaby, munching a sandwich and eyeing the lunchtime crowd, "that Rigby is important."

"What about Cranston's sleeve and so on?"

"I'll ask him about that when he comes in a minute, but I shall be surprised if we don't end up talking about Rigby. The Ashe-Ferrers-Plummer entanglement is the only area where Rigby's name doesn't appear."

"I don't suppose Wolfe knew him."

"No, I suppose not. I want to know where Wolfe is. The last time we couldn't find someone when we wanted him he ended up dead. There's no Rigby link with Duncan-Smith either. Sandwich?"

124

Barnaby pushed the plate of sandwiches across the table. Arnold chose one with care, then took a pull at his tankard. He was enjoying working with Barnaby.

As if reading his thoughts, Barnaby said, "I shall be leaving you on your own tomorrow. You can probably guess where I'm going."

"Devon—to see Mrs. Rigby at Kentisbury Ford."

"Exactly. I'm glad you're so well attuned. It gives me confidence to leave you in charge here. Ah, here's Professor Cranston."

He stood up as Cranston picked his way through the drinkers. In this aggressively male setting he carried a fastidious air not apparent before. When he spoke, there was an underlying tension in his voice, though his manner was not unfriendly.

"I'm not used to meeting people in hostelries, Inspector, but I received your message and I'm sure it's important."

"Good of you to come, Professor, and I shan't keep you long. Did you see Mr. Brereton on your way here? I hoped he might be able to come, too."

"No. He wasn't at lunch. I believe he was lecturing this morning, but I haven't seen him."

"In that case he probably didn't get my message, so we won't wait for him. Do sit down."

Cranston eyed the two policemen shrewdly, waiting for them to speak.

"I want to know about the confidential files, Professor," opened Barnaby. "I understand the Senior Tutor is responsible for them before they're handed over to the Bursar for storage. How safe are they?"

"Safer than they used to be. When Paxton was Senior Tutor—he was my predecessor, a very vague historian—he just kept them in an unlocked cupboard in his rooms. Then there was all that trouble at provincial universities in the sixties. I expect you remember it. Students complaining that there shouldn't be any confidential files and saying the authorities had secret dossiers on them. In one or two cases they actually got hold of the files and used them to make a fuss. We decided we had to tighten up. I still keep the files in my study, but they're always under lock and key—and so are my rooms."

"And you've never given access to anyone other than a Fellow?"

"Certainly not."

"Not even"—Barnaby paused—"not even Burgess?"

Cranston's gaze was steady. "Below the belt, Inspector. That was a confidence which is irrelevant to your case. But to answer you, no, not even Burgess."

"You can't play according to the Queensberry Rules in murder, Professor. And every undergraduate has a file—there are no exceptions?"

"No. A file is opened when a candidate applies to the College. It just has confidential reports from schools, information on family circumstances—broken homes and so on. There isn't much in some of them. Certainly nothing sinister."

"Do many Fellows want to see the files?"

"No. Once the undergraduate has been accepted by the College they're hardly looked at again unless some sort of personal problem develops. Luffman goes through them all in his capacity as Chaplain at the start of the academic year."

"When did you become Senior Tutor?"

"1974."

"Following Paxton?"

"Yes."

"Which means that Paxton was responsible for the files when Rigby was here. Would you expect Paxton to remember if any files were missing in his day?"

"No. He's dead."

"Dead?"

"He went on a lecture tour to the U.S. about five years ago, and he was killed when his 707 crashed near Kennedy Airport."

"So there's no means of knowing whether the file went to the Bursar or not. It could have been removed before or after Paxton retired."

"I suppose so. In those days we didn't worry too much about files. Even if Paxton were alive, I doubt if he'd remember."

"To your knowledge, Professor, did anyone show any interest in Ashe's file?"

"He was an undergraduate before I became Senior Tutor. He was older than he looked, you know. He'd been a Fellow for nearly ten years, though he still managed to mix with the undergraduates. But I do know that the Master sent for his file at the time we were considering what to do about his influence in the College. That was just after Rigby had lost his Fellowship. I happen to know because I took it over to the Lodge for him, and we actually looked at it together. But having told you that, Inspector, I must also say that it can't have any possible connection with the case."

"You must allow me to judge that, Professor."

"Perhaps I may be allowed a question. Why should anyone want Rigby's file? His record before he came to Beaufort was exemplary in every way. It was only after he got here that things went wrong."

"A fair question, Professor," said Barnaby. "To which I hope shortly to provide an answer."

Cranston was relaxing. He ran a hand ruminatively around his chin, then back over the dome of his head. Barnaby noticed the diagonal scratch running from the base of his thumb to the inside of his wrist.

"The trouble with all this upheaval in the College, Inspector," opined Cranston, "is that our meals are rushed. I'm not blaming you, of course—I know you're only doing your job—but I had to leave lunch before the pudding. Might I have one of your sandwiches?"

127

"Go ahead, sir, go ahead."

Arnold pushed the plate toward Cranston. Again the hand stretched out and the line of dried blood was revealed.

"There is just one thing, Professor. Forgive me for mentioning it, but you seem to have scratched your hand."

Cranston finished his mouthful of sandwich. "Yes, it was an awkward cut. I caught it on the inside of my car door and bled like a pig for half an hour." He smiled. "It's all this business of safety belts, you know. With anyone of my build they're tricky to put on and off, and when you're in a hurry you do silly things. I find it difficult enough getting in and out of the car itself these days. Ah, thank you, Sergeant." He stretched for the last sandwich.

❧

"There aren't so many B's," said Miss Crisp brightly.

Sparshott-Heyhoe, plotting on his map someone called Badger living opportunely in Brockenhurst, said nothing.

"Ah, Sir Michael Braine," said Miss Crisp, waving a card. "He's the Master of the College, isn't he? Why is he here? I thought these were people who had been through the College as undergraduates."

"No. Everyone's here—Fellows and undergraduates."

"Now, Brigadier, what do I do about the dons—do we send them the Appeal literature?"

"As a matter of fact, you've put your finger on a sensitive point. It's always debatable whether those who work for an institution should be asked for money as well as those who attend it. When I run a campaign I leave them out. As far as I'm concerned, they do their duty by working for the College, and if they do that conscientiously it's something of an insult to ask them for money as well. That's the way I look at it, though I know there are some managers who disagree. But they risk upsetting the very people who are going to provide the names of likely organisers and who will make the first approach. No. We leave them out."

128

"How shall I know who they are? I only know Braine because he's the Master."

With resignation, Sparshott-Heyhoe laid down his pen and reached behind him for the *Beaufort College Register*. "I'll read out the names and you take out the cards. For example" —he turned to the page listing the Fellows—"the next one will be Brereton, the Senior Fellow."

"Braine, Brakspear, Bramham, Brander, Brass-Cooper, Bratton-Burdett, Bravo, Brendon, Brett—that's odd, Brigadier. Are you sure Brereton is next? There's no card here."

"There ought to be. Try the next—Cowper."

She thumbed through the cards, inexorably reading out each name as she passed it. "Yes, here we are—Cowper, Julian."

"Then Cranston and Duncan-Smith."

"Poor old man. Not much point in asking him for anything now." She took out the two cards. "Next, sir?"

Slowly they went through the list, removing each of the Fellows. At the end the Brigadier shut the register and looked across at his secretary. "Now, Miss Crisp, perhaps we can get on with those who *will* contribute something."

He stood up in front of the map, his hand poised with a small red flag representing a Beaufort man who was a Lord Lieutenant and might be expected to organise the social side of the Appeal in one of the remoter shires. But he did not put it into the map. Instead he paused and wondered why Brereton's card was not with the others. It was probably just an administrative untidiness, a minor clerical error, the incompetent work of someone else's Miss Crisp. Yet it was odd.

Sparshott-Heyhoe was not the man to be waylaid by trivialities, but he did not forget small unexplained discrepancies either. Mentally he filed it away. Then he pushed the Lord Lieutenant firmly into the county town and looked round for the flag of one of the few Beaufort men who had made a mark for himself in industry and now headed a multinational company. Under his breath he said, "We could do with a few more of these."

❧

The rain had stopped but the low scudding clouds brought a premature twilight; in the High the shop fronts glowed brightly, the pavements glistened; in Beaufort the wrought-iron wall lamps were turned on early, making a pattern in Fletcher Quad, a counterpoint to the lights in the chapel, the library, and undergraduate rooms.

In his study on the second floor, Cranston looked out at the darkened rectangle of the quad before pulling the curtains. For a man of sedentary habits he was moving with uncharacteristic speed and sense of purpose. He glanced at some papers on his desk before tearing them up and throwing them in the fire. He opened a drawer, took out a cheque book, and put it into his inside pocket. He went to his bedroom and began to fill the suitcase lying on the bed. Socks, clean shirt, change of underclothes, pyjamas, shaving kit, towel, slippers, and dressing gown. Cranston packed them quickly but tidily. Back in the study he took his ignition keys from the mantelpiece, put on a heavy overcoat, picked up the suitcase, and after a final glance round the room, turned out the light, shut the door, and locked it behind him.

Outside he paused on the landing as though considering whether he had left anything behind; then he put on his hat and, quietly for a man so heavily built, went down the stairs. At the bottom he paused again, this time almost conspiratorially, looking left and right in the cloister before hastening away to the postern gate.

CHAPTER 18

WHEN he left the Eastgate, Barnaby spent the afternoon tying up loose ends. He confirmed that ties of the type used to kill Ashe were no longer available except to special order. The firm in Halifax said no order had been made within the last six years. The last one had been from Trumpers, the long-established High Street tailor. But informal trends in undergraduate dress had been the kiss of death for several such institutions and Trumpers was no more. Barnaby managed to track down one of their erstwhile salesmen serving in a wine supermarket. He had a vague memory of Sir Michael Braine buying a tie, but beyond that the information ran out. Barnaby then saw the Master, who readily admitted buying such a tie some four years previously, shortly before Trumpers's demise; he also said he had recommended them to several of his colleagues. Braine seemed not in the least disturbed by the enquiry—indeed, he found it mildly amusing. For the moment the tie was inconclusive.

Leaving the Master's Lodge, he went straight to Holywell to make another attempt to see Caroline Ferrers. This time she was in and opened the door to him wearing dark blue trousers and a white sweater; her blonde hair swung rhythmically as she turned her head. Rather like a model in a shampoo commercial, thought Barnaby.

"Come in, Inspector. I've been expecting you." She showed him into an upstairs sitting-room where he had apparently interrupted her at a typewriter.

"Are you an undergraduate, Miss Ferrers?"

She smiled: a confident, tolerant smile that might have annoyed him had he been a younger man who valued the opinion of a pretty girl. "No, but I like the academic atmosphere."

"I don't want to be rude, but how do you make your living?"

"Typing mostly, free-lance." She indicated the typewriter. "There are hundreds of theses that need typing. They're almost mass-produced these days, you know. You'd be surprised at the subjects I've covered. Everything from 'Baltic Naval Supplies in the Seventeenth Century' to 'The Mating Habits of the Orkney Vole.' It's an extraordinary industry, but it pays me reasonably."

"And you have good contacts."

Ferrers's eyes widened a fraction. "I had no idea policemen had a sense of humour, Inspector. Yes, as you say, I have my contacts."

Barnaby shifted uncomfortably in the small chair he had been offered by the window and ran his eyes around the room. It was simply but elegantly furnished in a combination of orange and brown; there were a lot of potted plants, and the longest wall was dominated by a painting of a deformed fish.

"Comfortable, but unpretentious," said Ferrers, following his appraising glance.

"I'm sorry, Miss Ferrers, my professional scrutiny," said Barnaby. "I'd better get to the point. I understand from Mr. Plummer that you spent the night of Duncan-Smith's death in Beaufort. He told me in confidence, and I said there would be no need for anyone else to know unless it proved

132

to be materially connected with the murder. Plummer was reluctant to mention your presence at all, but I think he felt it better to let me know openly rather than have me discover it for myself. He was anxious to shield you."

"Jonathan's very old-fashioned."

"And you're very emancipated?"

"You could say that. I don't suppose I have much of a virginal reputation to lose. What I meant was that he made a contrast to David—David Ashe. I expect you've heard me mentioned in connection with him, too."

It suddenly occurred to Barnaby that she might not yet know of Ashe's death. He said, "When did you last see Ashe?"

"When he walked out of this flat. He'd been living here until he discovered Jonathan and I were having an affair."

"Have you heard about him?"

"Yes. Jonathan told me."

Barnaby watched her closely. The only hint of emotion was a tightening of the muscles at the side of her mouth, pulling her lips into a taut line.

"Were you sorry?"

"No."

"Not at all?"

"I had come to hate him. Earlier this week I could have killed him myself."

During this exchange Caroline Ferrers seemed to alter. No longer was she a carefree, flippant girl leading an easygoing life; now there was an indefinable toughness, a thread of steel.

She repeated her words slowly. "I could have killed him myself."

"But you didn't."

"No. I told you. I didn't see him after he left here."

"Let's start at the beginning. What time did you go to the College that night?"

"Some time after nine. I had supper here. Jonathan had asked me to come over after Hall." .

"Did you go in by the main entrance?"

"No. Jonathan gave me his key to the postern. I went straight up to his rooms, put on a record, and waited for him."

"No one knew you were there except Plummer?"

"Exactly."

"Forgive me asking this, but why did you keep it a secret? It's not a crime to have a lady in one's rooms."

"Women aren't meant to stay all night, though a lot do. We had already decided I should do that."

"Why?" Barnaby waved a hand. "What's wrong with the comforts of your own flat here?"

Ferrers smiled again, a private smile. "Men are still little boys at heart, Inspector. Even stuffy old Fellows of Oxford Colleges. Jonathan had tasted the forbidden fruits here—he thought they might taste sweeter if he broke the rules of the College. The whole setup still has a monastic aura even now, and I gather there's something rather naughty about having a girl in one's rooms all night. If that sounds a bit naïve, I can assure you that *I* felt very wicked being there. I kept imagining that a porter in a bowler hat would break into Johnny's rooms and have me carried out. To be honest, I got a mild thrill out of it, too."

"Did you see anyone on your way to his rooms?"

"I think I passed an undergraduate on the stairs, but it wasn't anyone I knew."

"You relocked the postern?"

"It locks itself. Although it's a big door it just has a Yale lock for convenience."

"And once you were in Plummer's rooms you saw no one?"

"I must be careful. I want to tell you the whole truth— Johnny told me to." Again she smiled spontaneously, her most attractive feature.

"Very wise, Miss Ferrers," said Barnaby pompously, feeling not for the first time that the interviewing of attractive young women called for skills he did not possess. He looked out of the window where the lights of New College shone across the street. A heavy lorry changed gear outside, its engine throbbing through the buildings pressing close on either side.

"I waited in Johnny's room until he came in from Hall. It must have been shortly after ten—I can't be more exact than that. He told me he'd have a quick glass of port in the Common Room and then he'd be able to get away without seeming rude because there were a lot of living-out Fellows dining. As he's Junior Fellow it's a sort of tradition that he pours the second cup of coffee—the first is served by the butler, who's allowed to go off duty. I gather David Ashe always refused to pour the coffee when he was Junior Fellow. In fact he often didn't go in to dinner at all. Anyway, Johnny poured the coffee and came away. I should like to think he hurried over."

"Just so," said Barnaby, looking past her at the fish on the wall.

"Once he got back to his rooms he stayed put. We listened to records and mulled a bottle of claret. Neither of us went out again. Some time before midnight we looked out of the window when we heard a disturbance over by the library. It must have been shortly after the old man's body was discovered. At the time we didn't know that, and as we saw Group Captain Farquhar there, we thought it was something to do with the manuscript."

"You heard a disturbance?"

"Yes. People talking, running feet, that sort of thing. But it was fun looking out of the window." Again that smile. "You see, Inspector, I hadn't many clothes on at the time. There was the stuffy old College and here were we in the warm security of Johnny's room. Rather like looking out at a snowstorm on a winter's day with a roaring log fire inside. Our little world was private to us."

Barnaby was hauling himself to his feet as though he had not heard. "So you saw nothing that might help us. And next morning?"

"Next morning I found the postern guarded by a large

policeman, so I had to go out by the main gate. The porter looked at me in an odd way, but he's a nice old thing with an eye for a pretty girl and I didn't think he'd say anything. Besides, there are always girls there, so it wasn't new for him. As far as I know, he's the only person apart from you who knows I was there. For Johnny's sake, I'd rather it stayed that way."

"Ashe didn't know?"

She shook her head. "No, I certainly didn't see him, and I've no reason to believe he saw me. And Johnny wouldn't have told him."

Barnaby reached the door, bending his head under the lintel. "I just wanted to be sure about that because it looks as though he may have been killed at the same time as Duncan-Smith."

"But I thought he was found at the station?"

"People do not always die where they are found, Miss Ferrers—at least not those who are murdered. However, if you're certain you didn't see him, and if you're equally certain Mr. Plummer was with you the whole time, then there is no problem as far as you two are concerned."

He made as if to go out, then said, "Oh, there is one thing, Miss Ferrers. Did you ever hear Mr. Plummer talk about someone called Rigby?"

Her eyes flicking momentarily to the fish gave her away. "He may have. Was he at the College? Jonathan mentions a lot of names."

"But it wasn't a name to which he attached any importance?"

"Well, it certainly didn't make a mark with me."

But it did, thought Barnaby—there's something there. And he had the feeling that the balance of the interview had been redressed. He stood up. "No, don't bother to see me out."

He went down the stairs two at a time. As he did so he wondered what that moment of confusion had revealed. Surprise? Guilt? Or merely the bewilderment of one unused to dealings with the police?

He let himself out into Holywell Street. At the far end, in Longwall Street, the late afternoon rush-hour traffic already stretched back in an irregular line of shining metal, red lights, and steaming exhausts.

❦

Cranston wished he had left earlier. He had already been caught in a jam in the High and now he found himself wedged between a taxi and a furniture van in the area of the station. His elderly Vauxhall, temporarily relieved of the need to exert itself, murmured gently. He took advantage of the delay to wipe his spectacles and those parts of the steamed-up windscreen within reach.

The taxi ahead of him, yellow indicator flashing, pulled sharply across the stream of oncoming traffic and cleared his path. He let in the clutch and pulled away down the Botley Road. On Cumnor Hill he was held up behind an oil tanker, but he was able to overtake it at the top. As he drew clear of the city lights, the road to Faringdon lay damp and empty before him. Carefully he pressed the accelerator and the speedometer moved up to fifty miles an hour. At that point he held the needle steady and eased himself into a more relaxed position. He settled down for a long drive.

❦

As Barnaby climbed the steps at the Beaufort entrance, Barker called out to him from the Lodge, "Inspector Barnaby, sir! Have you a moment, please?"

Barnaby went into the Lodge where Barker was sorting post. An old-fashioned oil stove was smelling strongly.

Barker leaned forward confidentially. "I'm glad you're back, sir. I had the American gentleman in here a little while ago—Professor Wolfe. He was looking for you and was in a bit of a state. I told him I thought you'd be back soon, and he went off back to his rooms. But he said I should tell you particularly that he wants to see you. Tell the Inspector, he said, that it's a matter of real importance. And he was looking worried, too, sir. If I was you, sir . . ."

"Right," said Barnaby in the crisp style he adopted when he saw action ahead of him. "How long ago was this?"

"About ten minutes, sir, perhaps a bit longer."

"Where are his rooms?"

"Lancaster Hall, second staircase, Room Five, sir. We put the Americans in there because it's got Tudor panelling. They like that, you know."

The approach to Lancaster Hall, the only remaining part of the medieval College, was through a small Gothic arch whose deceptive height had caught many an undergraduate a resounding blow. Barnaby was suitably circumspect and bent himself low. Inside were uneven steps rising to an oak-panelled gallery from which three staircases twisted upward; on the right-hand wall name boards announced the occupants of the rooms.

Wolfe's rooms were on the top floor. On the landing outside his door a mullioned window looked out on a small paved quadrangle, the most central area of the College where, on a warm summer's day before examinations, undergraduates seeking peace work in cool seclusion; now, on a damp October evening, the leaded lights of the window revealed only decaying leaves and wet flagstones. Before he could knock, the door to his right opened, and Wolfe himself emerged. He was jacketless, in a dark blue shirt and matching tie. But it was his face that held Barnaby's attention. His pallor was acute and beneath his rimless spectacles grey shadows highlighted the bone structure of his face, making him drawn and strained.

"Thank God you've come, Inspector." His drawl was emphasised by his air of fatigue. "Please come in and sit down."

The room, decorated in magnolia and discreetly lit by

table lamps, was restful and contrasted with the sense of strain shown by its occupant. Three bars of an electric fire ensured a warm transatlantic temperature. Barnaby sat down in a low armchair; Wolfe remained standing and moved nervously around the room as he spoke.

"I've been holding out on you, Inspector, and I haven't any excuse, except that I didn't want to get involved. I'm a guest here, you see, and I've been well treated by everybody. Real English hospitality, you know. I didn't want to interfere, to hurt anyone. But I've been worried stiff, Mr. Barnaby, ever since Duncan-Smith was killed. I expect you've been looking for me, but I've been staying with an American friend in Balliol, hiding, you might say. You see"—he pushed his fingers through his hair—"I was in the library when it happened."

There it was, blunt and uncomplicated. And yet if he expected any reaction from Barnaby, he was disappointed.

Wolfe bent forward over the back of the settee. He repeated, "I was in the library. I heard it happen."

Barnaby stirred. "Heard?"

"I was down in the stack-room underneath the main hall. I'm working on a study of corruptions of medieval texts, and I'd gone to check an early edition of *Piers Plowman*. I was at the bottom of the stairs that come down from the main hall when I heard a disturbance upstairs. I wasn't really listening, but the library is usually so quiet that any noise out of the ordinary catches the attention. I couldn't tell you what it was, Mr. Barnaby, but it sounded like books dropping on the floor —quite a lot of books. Anyway, I just assumed someone had tripped and dropped what he was carrying. I didn't go up— no one cried out."

Wolfe had become animated and some colour had come back into his face. He went on. "After that, not long after, I heard the old professor, Duncan-Smith. He had a high voice, you know, and it carried. He said, 'Hullo, J. C.,' as though someone he knew had come up to him. It was quite clear—

139

then there was a heavy noise. It wasn't books this time. I couldn't think what it was. Since then I've wondered if it might have been"—he blinked and paused—"if it might have been a body falling on the floor."

Barnaby remained silent, watching the American over the tips of his fingers.

"At the time it meant nothing to me at all. There was no reason to suppose anything was wrong. Besides, other people were up there. I heard the door open and shut several times, and there was whispering—the sort of whispering you get in a library. I don't know how many people, but there was quite a lot of moving about, footsteps to and fro. In the end I thought everybody had gone, but the door opened again a bit later as though someone had come back. Eventually, the door went for the last time—you can't mistake it—and after that I felt that the library was empty. I wasn't really concentrating; I can't be absolutely certain about the order of events.

"I worked for another five minutes or so, then went back up to the main hall. Thinking about it afterwards, I guess I was uneasy the moment I got up there. There was a light on in the nearest bay—and you know what I found. The Professor was sitting in the chair with his head thrown back. I'd gotten used to seeing him asleep, but this time something was different. He didn't look natural."

"What did you do?"

"Nothing," he said hoarsely. "Nothing at all. I knew I was suspect over the letter and now, within those few seconds, I sensed—I can't put it stronger than that—I sensed I was in the middle of something that could do me nothing but harm. Duncan-Smith looked *dead*; I had heard strange sounds. Quite simply, I was frightened. I saw my whole year at Oxford in ruins. I'm ashamed, Mr. Barnaby, awfully ashamed. I acted like a coward. I left the library as quickly and quietly as I could. I touched nothing—I just came away. And since then I've had no sleep. This afternoon I came to my senses. I heard just about everything that evening and my holding out on you was plain stupid. That's it, Mr. Barnaby. That's the whole truth, so help me God."

Wolfe looked exhausted and sat down. Barnaby wasted no time with recrimination. He said, "I want to check one or two points. Duncan-Smith said, 'Hullo, J. C.' Is that it?"

"Right. He said it in that confident way he had." Wolfe laughed almost hysterically. "It was always funny when he got the wrong person. He could be so vague. I don't think he ever knew who I was at all."

"And you could distinguish no individual voice in the whispering you heard?"

"No—I guess not."

"Books dropping, heavy fall, perhaps of a body, whispering, the library door several times. Is that it?"

"I reckon that sums it up."

"And there was nothing else—nothing else at all?"

"No—well—there was one thing."

"Go on."

"I hesitate to mention it, Mr. Barnaby, because I'm not even sure I heard it. But while I was standing at the bottom of the stairs, once during the whispering and again at the end, just before the door shut for the last time, I thought I heard a double metallic click."

"A double metallic click?"

"Perhaps a triple click would describe it more accurately. Like this: *click-pause-click-click*. Not loud, and I'm not even sure I heard it twice, but I think I did. It was more an impression than a concrete sound. But that was the rhythm of it: *click-pause-click-click*." Wolfe put his hand to his head. "I guess I'm not being much use to you, Mr. Barnaby. I find it difficult to be certain of anything now. The harder you try to bring back the details . . ."

Barnaby stood up. "That's all for now, Mr. Wolfe. You'd better get some rest. I'm glad you've had the sense to come forward at last."

"You know what worries me now, don't you, Mr. Barnaby?

Suppose the old man wasn't dead when I saw him. I may have missed the chance of getting medical help, of saving his life. My selfishness, my cowardice is quite inexcusable."

"I don't think you need worry yourself on that score, sir. All our evidence suggests that Duncan-Smith's death was instantaneous."

Barnaby left without further comment and went out into Fletcher Quad. To himself he said, "Bloody American idiot. Let's hope we're pointing in the right direction now. *At least two people, possibly more. Click-pause-click-click.* And '*Hullo, J. C.*' Julian Cowper? James Cranston?"

The time was six o'clock, and it was raining again. Cranston turned on the wipers and leaned forward to peer through the windscreen. He crested a small wooded eminence and dipped his headlights as he drove down the hill into the ancient borough of Faringdon.

CHAPTER 19

BARNABY went back to the lecture room, where various reports were now available. The full fingerprint report on the library told him little or nothing. Prints on the door handles and tables were numerous and much as might have been expected. The disarranged Pitt and Fox books had Brereton's and Miss Jarvis's prints, but that was hardly surprising. The peace badge had Ashe's prints, apparently confirming Plummer's view that it was his. The more he thought about it, the more he inclined to the opinion that Ashe had been killed in the library, though he had to admit that Wolfe's picture of partly heard events contributed confusion rather than clarity.

What were the voices he had heard? Could there have been collusion after all? And that crucial "Hullo, J. C." That could point in only two directions, and for the moment both were baffling. But how reliable was Duncan-Smith? Suppose his identification was faulty, as it often was. If only he could link Rigby with Duncan-Smith, he felt he might have the connection that would give the key to the whole business. He could not believe the old man's killing was as motiveless as it appeared. He looked at his watch, realised there was not time to see Plummer before Hall, and went off to his room to change.

During his enquiries at the College, Barnaby had tried to avoid too much social contact with the dons. He never moved easily in company, and he found it doubly difficult knowing he was viewed as a policeman on duty whose every remark would be searched for a hidden meaning. Nevertheless, the Master had given him a standing invitation to dine, and he had decided to take advantage of it before leaving for the West Country. Besides, he wanted to see Plummer and hoped to catch him over a drink in the Senior Common Room.

The Common Room was full, and he was immediately welcomed by the Master, who saw him come in. A log fire was burning, and the maroon curtains added to the atmosphere of warmth and comfort. Braine poured a sherry from a Georgian decanter and shepherded Barnaby towards a Fellow he had not met before, a man with a Habsburg chin and lugubrious expression.

"Inspector, you must meet Dr. Gibbs, our tutor in law. I sometimes think it's good for the men of theory to meet the men of practice. What do you say, Gibbs?"

Gibbs produced a smile of conventional friendliness, folded his gown carefully about him, and steered a stilted conversation away from the subject uppermost in their minds. Barnaby listened with half an ear and made the occasional remark when it was expected of him, but he was looking over Gibbs's shoulder, hoping Plummer would arrive early enough for a word before dinner. Plummer did not materialise, but Cowper, looking more relaxed than usual and therefore hiding, Barnaby deduced, a heightened nervousness, came into the room and poured himself a drink. He saw Barnaby and crossed over.

"Picking the brains of our shrewd Gibbs, Inspector? He must be one of the few men you can't suspect. You wouldn't know it to look at him, but he has numerous progeny and lives in a vast Victorian villa in North Oxford. On the night in question I'm sure he was in the bosom of his family and far from the scene of the crime."

144

Gibbs coughed, a dry, harsh sound. "I'm surprised, Cowper, that you were here either," he remarked acidly. "I had formed the impression that you had a nightly engagement on the television. I am frequently astonished that you have opinions on so many subjects."

Cowper shrugged off the calculated sneer with an easy laugh. "The original polymath, Gibbs. In an age of specialisation I still embody Newman's idea of a liberal education. None of your two cultures for me."

"You specialised on the Wansdyke," observed Barnaby.

"Ah, yes, Inspector. An historian must have one field in which he is the undisputed authority—if only to maintain his self-esteem."

At this point Barnaby saw Plummer arrive, but before he could get hold of him Wilson announced dinner, and the Fellows filed into Hall. They processed between tables of silent undergraduates up to High Table, and a Latin grace was enunciated by a youth with bifocals and a whistling impediment in his speech. The Dean, playing host with an air of calculation that somehow removed all spontaneity, ushered Barnaby to a favoured position between himself and Luffman, with the Master sitting opposite.

"Another full house tonight," said Braine, unfolding his napkin and surveying the table. "If you will not think me flippant, Inspector, I must tell you that our colleagues have appeared at the evening rites with much more diligence since we acquired our notoriety."

"They don't want to miss the gossip," said Luffman. "It hasn't made them any more assiduous in attending chapel. There was a congregation of six at Evensong and that included me." Luffman threw his remark into the middle of the table as though indifferent to its effect. The bitterness of his tone was unmistakable.

"You'll have to liven up the services, Quentin," said Braine. "There'll need to be some justification for your existence when we spend the money the Brigadier is raising for your dry rot." His bantering tone was meant to rally Luff-man; at the same time, he had pulled Sparshott-Heyhoe, who was sitting on his right, into the conversation.

"Compulsory church parade would do it, Master," said the Brigadier. "But I expect that's out of date. Hardly do it in the army now, you know. And I can't say I'm sorry. I remember the days when we prayed by numbers. Mind you, it was different during the war. Then people wanted to pray. Do you know, on the way to the beach on D-Day I saw men pray as I've never seen before or since. I remember talking to one private in the Somersets." He broke off, aware that conversation had stopped around him. "I'm sorry, Master. There's no bore like a war bore. You mustn't let me get started."

"Not at all, Brigadier. Personally I think we all forget the war too easily. Natural enough, of course, for the present generation, they don't want to live in the past. But we ought to be aware of what we nearly lost—I don't think a lot of people are. And if they're not, then up to a point we are to blame because we are the educators."

Farquhar, on Sparshott-Heyhoe's right, spoke for the first time. "Did you ever hear Ashe talking about the war?"

Another awkward hiatus followed. Eyes flickered in Barnaby's direction, then down to the soup.

Braine took his handkerchief from his shirtcuff—keeping it there was an affectation copied from an erstwhile Master of Balliol—and held it to his nose before returning it with a flourish. Luffman and Sparshott-Heyhoe both spoke at once and in the ensuing apologies and counterapologies Barnaby turned quietly to Cowper.

"I don't suppose you know why there isn't a file for Rigby in the Bursar's records, do you?"

Cowper continued the motion of applying the soupspoon to his mouth, dabbed his lips with his napkin, and then replied at the same volume level. "No, Inspector, I've no idea.

Mind you, I expect even the best filing systems break down from time to time."

"No doubt, no doubt."

"I wonder if you'll have time to attend the Dryburgh Lecture tomorrow, Inspector," broke in Braine, unaware that he was interrupting. "It's one of the highlights of the academic year and Brereton has been elected. He doesn't seem to be dining tonight, so I expect he's working on the text. He's always a perfectionist. Puts the rest of us to shame, doesn't he, Julian?"

The Master looked round the table. Barnaby did likewise and suddenly realised that Brereton was not alone in his absence. Cranston was not there. An intuitive alarm bell sounded in that area of his consciousness reserved for such things. In the short time he had known him he was not aware that Cranston had ever missed a meal.

Braine was going on. "His subject is somewhat esoteric—to do with the Marcher Lords, I understand—but he's bound to be entertaining. Rumour has it that he intends to destroy a theory propounded by the Regius Professor. A Fellow of Keble once resigned his Fellowship after being taken apart publicly by Brereton."

Politely, but absentmindedly, for he was still thinking of Cranston, Barnaby said, "Yes, Sir Michael, I should like to come—if it doesn't take too long."

"About an hour, Inspector. It depends on how long the demolition of his colleagues takes, before he gets onto his own thesis."

"I should be able to manage that. I shall be leaving Oxford for a short while when it's over."

Barnaby hoped he did not sound curt. But he felt time running out and he already regretted coming to dinner. In the few seconds since he had noticed it, Cranston's absence was assuming a significance of sizable proportions. Besides, although conversation was flowing smoothly enough all around him, he felt himself acting as an obstruction in the river; he sensed everyone listening when he spoke, partly out of respect for a guest, partly searching for a double meaning. So conscious was he of his isolation that he almost missed the Master's next remark.

"Yes, it's the highest accolade for an Oxford historian—we haven't had a Dryburgh here since John Redfern in the thirties, and he was a legendary figure."

"A contemporary of Duncan-Smith's," put in Gibbs dryly, entering the conversation for the first time. "They had rooms on the same staircase."

Mention of Duncan-Smith created another pause. Gibbs went on with his soup, noticing nothing.

The grey Vauxhall pulled clear of the suburbs of Swindon, crossed the M4, and headed southwest for Devizes. It was raining hard now, cutting diagonally across the headlights in glittering lines. Cranston stiffened as the car pulled up onto the Marlborough Downs, making a subconscious effort to help the straining engine, then relaxed as the road levelled off and he changed down. The wind swept across the exposed downland, throwing rain against the windscreen in gusts; the wipers faltered, then resumed their hypnotic beat.

He looked at his watch. Yes, he was doing well considering the weather. His eyes fell on the petrol gauge, and he realised the tank was almost empty. He drove for several miles and found a garage open on the edge of Avebury. A youth with lank hair left the warmth of his office and reluctantly put in six gallons. Cranston stayed in the car while the business was transacted, then restarted the engine and pulled back onto the A361. Ahead, through the rain, his lights picked out a huge shape, one of the Avebury sarsens, looming monstrously from the side of the road.

Dinner over, the Fellows retired to the Common Room, where Wilson served coffee and brandy or whisky. Barnaby, managing to get away from Cowper, found himself sitting between a zoologist, whose misfortune was to be totally deaf but who insisted on holding involved but necessarily one-sided conversations, and Sparshott-Heyhoe, who seemed pleased to have Barnaby near him. The Brigadier waited for a pause in the zoological monologue, then leaned over.

"I heard you mention a missing file. Was the name Rigby?"

Barnaby shifted his chair fractionally nearer. "Yes. Know anything about it?"

"No. But I've been going through the College address cards today and I'm missing one, too. I'd have forgotten about it if I hadn't overheard you at dinner."

"Who's missing?"

"Brereton."

"*Brereton*? Was he the only one?"

"I can't tell you about the undergraduates—it's difficult to check. But he was the only don. Probably only a clerical error. I've never met a completely flawless system. I wouldn't have thought of it again if you hadn't mentioned the file."

"Perhaps." Barnaby leaned nearer. "Have you seen Professor Cranston this evening?"

"He was at lunch. I sat next to him and got a lecture on the Oxford road system. He has strong views."

Barnaby nodded and looked at the semicircle of begowned figures. Plummer was circulating with the coffeepot. "Quite a lot of them have strong views, but they're mostly theorists and would fly a mile if they had to face reality. I've got to find the one who had the strength of mind to put his views into practise."

On his right the zoologist came back to life. "I don't suppose, Inspector," he said, "that you are conversant with the life history of the Large Blue?"

149

Cranston drove carefully through Avebury, circumnavigated the roundabout where the A361 crosses the A4, and set off on the long straight stretch to Devizes. Ahead, a chain of headlights marked the course of the road over the Downs. In the darkness, crawling up Morgan's Hill and All Canning's Down, the Wansdyke lay silent and unseen on each side of the road.

Cranston's foot remained steady on the accelerator. Doing a steady fifty, he drove on through the night.

CHAPTER 20

BARNABY declined another whisky, excused himself to Sparshott-Heyhoe, the zoologist, and the Master, and left the Common Room. While nodding his head at what he took to be the right moments in the saga of the Large Blue, he had been considering certain aspects of the case.

First, he was beginning to feel a sense of urgency; Cranston's absence could well be dangerous. Then he wondered about the Bursar's record system and decided Arnold would have to check it while he was away. If there were other flaws, the absence of Rigby's file and Brereton's card might be seen as part of an overall pattern of inefficiency; if not . . . And Luffman was worrying him. He had watched him closely during dinner, and, if ever a man was headed for a nervous breakdown, it was Luffman. His tension had become more marked even in the short time he had known him. And men on the brink of a breakdown could not be regarded as responsible for their actions. Arnold would have to go through his account of the murder evening again.

Once away from the Common Room he went straight to Cranston's rooms and found them in darkness. At the Lodge Barker was on duty and said he had not seen the Professor since lunch. He checked his garage and the car had gone. "It's

151

odd, Inspector. He doesn't often go off in the term without letting us know."

Again, Barnaby felt the pulse of the case quickening. He did not forget that the last Fellow who had vanished had reappeared as a corpse. He went back to his room and got Arnold on the telephone. He gave general instructions to cover his absence, then said, "And find out if either Cowper or Cranston—or anyone else, I suppose—are ever referred to as 'J. C.' Do it discreetly—I don't want to stir up too much gossip in the Common Room. Then find Cranston. He's been out of the College since this afternoon. Get hold of him, find out where he's been, and tell him not to leave before I get back."

Arnold, at home with his wife and awakened from a sleep by the fire, gave monosyllabic answers to the quickfire instructions. He said, "Do you want me to see Broadhead again?"

"No. Don't waste time with him. But find out if there's any gossip in the Junior Common Room. Ashe had several links there and we've still got to find out how the remains of the manuscript were put in the post. Smell out the radical lot. Try some of Broadhead's friends. And do a detailed search of the Fellows' rooms. Don't upset them, but make sure they're thoroughly turned over."

"Difficult not to upset them."

"Just be tactful, that's all."

"Including the Master, sir?"

"Including the Master. And give Luffman a double check —I'm not happy about him. Then get hold of Wolfe and take him through every detail of the story he told me. I *think* he's all right, but I want to be certain. Besides, he might come up with something he left out. He was pretty shell-shocked when I saw him. Anyway, I'm off to Devon after this lecture tomorrow. I'll ring you in the evening to see if anything's come up."

After giving his orders, Barnaby paused for reflection. Although it went against all his preconceived notions, he was now more or less convinced that more than one person had been involved. The sheer size of the crate suggested it; then there was the whispering that Wolfe had heard. It could, of course, have taken place before the murders, but in view of the other noises it was unlikely. But there were two deaths. He could understand collusion in the killing of Ashe, he could even imagine a conspiracy with every Fellow involved from the Master downwards. But Duncan-Smith? He couldn't see one motive, let alone two.

He tried various permutations for a combination against Ashe, none wholly satisfactory. Cranston and Cowper? They seemed to have nothing in common at all; their fields were miles apart and it was difficult to imagine the extrovert Dean engaged in any enterprise with the staid professor of philology. Cowper and Brereton? The same applied, only more so. He could not see the Senior Fellow consorting for long with Cowper, much less carrying a crate with a corpse in it. Cranston and Braine, perhaps? That was more plausible— and they had admitted meeting on the night of the murders. But if so, why had Braine gone out of his way to tell him about Cranston's sleeve and scratch? An elaborate blind? He must never forget he was dealing with intelligent men.

The torn sleeve and the scratch. Suppose they had been acquired while carrying the crate, caught, perhaps, on a protruding nail? That looked promising. In that case "Hullo, J. C." must have been addressed to Cranston. If that was so, the Master must come into the reckoning. But what about Luffman as the accomplice? Suppose . . .

Mere speculation, no evidence. Necessary speculation, of course; his stock in trade. It was dangerous to start seeing Luffman as a religious fanatic, and he saw that coming up as the next step in the argument. But if he was on the verge of a breakdown . . . ?

And there was the curious sound Wolfe had heard, or thought he had heard. Click-pause-click-click. What credence should be given to that? Metallic, he'd said. He took two coins out of his pocket and knocked them together with the rhythm Wolfe had indicated. Click-pause-click-click. What did that suggest? Absolutely nothing. He did it again. No—it meant nothing at all. He returned the coins to his pocket and frowned. Although he was dissatisfied, he had indelibly etched the rhythm of the sound on his subconscious. He would recognise it if he heard it in the future.

He went back to the conspiracy theory. There was, of course, one combination that fitted together with no trouble at all. Plummer and Ferrers. A problem with "Hullo, J. C.," but after all it was well known that the old man got his names wrong more often than not. What looked like a good lead might in fact be quite the opposite.

He rang Barker at the Lodge and got himself put through to Plummer on the College phone.

"Sorry to disturb you so late, Mr. Plummer. I had hoped to catch you before dinner. Would you mind if I came round for a few minutes to see you now?"

"Can't it wait till tomorrow, Inspector?" Plummer's tone was discouraging without being unfriendly.

"Not really, sir."

"It's a quarter past ten, you know." The voice became querulous. "And I've several essays I must read before my tutorials start tomorrow. It really is very inconvenient."

"I'm sorry, sir. It's urgent."

"All right, Inspector."

Barnaby was intrigued by Plummer's curt manner. It occurred to him that Caroline Ferrers might be with him, but when he arrived in his sitting-room five minutes later he found him on his own, sitting in his shirt sleeves by a log fire.

"I hope we shan't be long, Inspector. I really must do some work. I've been putting it off all day."

"Not long, Mr. Plummer, if you tell me everything I want to know."

"An ambiguous remark, Inspector."

"When you spoke to me earlier, before Ashe's body was discovered, you said you could give me fifty motives for his death. I should like just one or two."

"Poetic license, Inspector. No one except his cronies liked him, as I expect you've discovered. In the Junior Common Room—he often went there—he acted as a sort of litmus paper, turning everyone red or blue, and you know what the Fellows thought. All the same, I can't see anyone disliking him enough to murder him."

"Someone did."

"Murder means hate."

"Certainly."

"Hate is personal, not theoretical."

"I agree."

"It's no good saying the Master killed him for the good of the College, or Brereton because he destroyed the letter. Incidentally, I take it Ashe did do that? It's a strong rumour. And his own little revolutionary clique of undergraduates says so."

"The evidence points that way." Barnaby was laconic; experience had taught him never to lose the initiative by allowing suspects to ask him questions. "No hate, then?"

Plummer looked straight at Barnaby. "Yes, I hated him."

Barnaby registered no emotion. "Not, presumably, because of the paint daubing. That doesn't come within the scope of your motive prospectus."

"No."

"Miss Ferrers?"

"Partly."

"Only partly?"

Plummer was staring into the fire. The logs were burning well; tongues of flame licked up the chimney.

"Inspector, have you heard the name Rigby mentioned?"

"Often."

155

"There you may find some hate. Perhaps enough for murder."

"I know about his death. And I know why certain people felt strongly about it."

"Not *felt*—*feel*, Inspector. It's important to get your tenses right in a pedantic academic institution. And when you're dealing with murder." He looked at Barnaby and then away again. "I'll tell you a story—and then perhaps I can get on with some work."

There was no mistaking the change in his manner. Barnaby said nothing but noted the tension underlying every word he spoke.

"There was once a frightened little boy who went away to boarding school. He'd never been away from home before and he was desperately homesick. All the rooms seemed so dark and cold, all the corridors so long. And he was bullied. To avoid the other boys he used to hide away in one of the remote form-rooms. There, in a corner, he read endlessly, and he made model aeroplanes—slowly and with infinite care. One day when he had just finished a model—it was a biplane, a Tiger Moth—three boys who had been watching its progress came in and took it. 'Time for a test flight,' said one. 'Let's see if it will loop the loop,' said another. The small boy protested and burst into tears. He watched out of a window as the plane was flown and broken. While he was crying at the window he felt someone in the room with him and a hand was put on his shoulder. It was a senior boy—only four years older, but a god by comparison. He comforted the small boy, got hold of the ones who had taken the plane and made them pay for it, and then he gave some good advice. He told the boy he wasn't helping himself by shutting himself away, that he should cut out the self-pity and start seeing what he could get out of the place. As a result of that advice the boy started playing games, discovered unsuspected talents, and eventually blossomed in the school in all sorts of ways. He ended up as Head of the School and Captain of Cricket."

156

The fire crackled unexpectedly. Barnaby said nothing.

"A romantic little story, Inspector. And you don't really need me to interpret it. As you've guessed, I was the small boy and Rigby was the boy who took pity on me and gave such sound advice. From that point on Terence Rigby was a sort of hero for me, and when I thought of the way he dealt with the bullies there was something deeper. I don't want to be sentimental about this—stiff upper lip, you know—but he became a sort of father figure. My own father was killed when I was young, so I'd never really had one. It sounds silly when I actually say it out loud, but that was the sort of relationship I felt it to be. He was a boy of principle, and as a miserable minnow in the school I respected him intensely. Difficult to say now, but perhaps I loved him."

Plummer stood up abruptly as though embarrassed. "Then you know what happened. We lost touch when he left Blundells—just occasionally I heard about him and I could see he was going to the top in the academic world. I put my own academic career on ice while I played some cricket for a year or two and eventually I was told what was happening to him. I tried to get him out of the commune he had joined, but it was too late. He was on heroin by then, and he died in squalor only a little while after I went to see him. Ashe had captured his idealism, perverted it, and ruined him.

"It was quite by chance that I was elected to my Fellowship at Beaufort. My own college was Queen's. Of course, once I got here I heard the whole background story and met Ashe. There you are, Inspector, it's as simple as that. You're only the third person I've told."

"Who were the others?" interjected Barnaby.

"James Cranston was the first. He was very fond of Terence. Nothing nasty, but I expect you've noticed his gay streak. He thinks no one sees that side of him, but actually it makes an able academic rather more human than he might otherwise be. The other was Julian Cowper. Terence and Julian did a lot of work together. I expect you know that, too. In fact, it was Terence's research that helped make Cowper's reputation with the Wansdyke article. To his credit, Cowper has always acknowledged that."

"Did you ever talk to Ashe about Rigby?"

"Only once."

"When was that?"

"Soon after I was elected. It was about the only time I spoke to him at all. It wasn't a row. I told him in about three sentences why he disgusted me. He didn't even reply."

"Did he know you were with Miss Ferrers?"

"No. He knew there was someone, but Caroline didn't let him know it was me. She's got a lot of friends and plenty of them are men. He didn't know I'd pushed him out."

"And that's how it was?"

"Yes, I don't think it's too arrogant to put it that way."

"The night of the murders, did you leave your rooms at all once Miss Ferrers had arrived?"

"No, neither of us did. We were aware of the disturbance by the library, but we didn't know about Duncan-Smith's death until the next morning."

"My last question, Mr. Plummer, and then I'll leave you. Your rooms look out onto Magpie Lane and they're the nearest to the postern. Did you hear a car in the·lane that night? Or any unusual noise at all? It could have been in the small hours."

Plummer, who had been standing with his back to the fire, sat down. Much of the tension had gone out of him.

"Inspector, I don't want to shock you, but you seem to forget that I was otherwise engaged."

Barnaby smiled, a small smile. "So I understand, sir. Then I will repeat one question. Are you quite certain that neither of you left the College that night?"

Plummer enunciated his words slowly and clearly. "Quite certain, Inspector. Quite certain."

"And there's nothing else?"

"No—nothing." He hesitated. "Nothing—except . . ."

"Go on."

"It was the night of the murder, or rather earlier in the evening, that James Cranston behaved so oddly at the Dunstable. He was very worked up about something—I thought he was losing control of himself. Subsequently, I came to the conclusion it was connected with the boy soloist, but I could have been wrong. Anyway, I was worried about him—shocked might be a better word—and when I bumped into Brereton I thought I ought to tell him. He's Senior Fellow and very much of Cranston's generation. I went up to his rooms with him, but he didn't seem able to concentrate on what I was saying. It was like talking to a man in a dream. Later I rationalised it by saying he was worrying about the letter, but I'm sure it was more than that. Normally he'd have taken an interest in a colleague, but he just didn't say anything. He was totally preoccupied."

"Has he been normal since?"

"More or less. He's an angular fellow at the best of times and finds it difficult to get close to people. But he makes an effort, and if you can get through the reserve, there's a warm centre. He was very welcoming when I first came to the College. That's why I spoke to him about Cranston. I thought he'd be sympathetic."

"Thank you, Mr. Plummer. Now I'll leave you to your work. I'm sorry to have taken up so much of your time."

Plummer was conciliatory. "Sorry I was short just now. The fact is I ought to have done the work earlier in the day. Let me know if there's any other way you think I can help."

"I will, Mr. Plummer, I certainly will."

As Barnaby made his way down the staircase from Plummer's rooms, Cranston reached the outskirts of Taunton. The streets glistened, but the rain had stopped and the night was clear. He passed the County Cricket Ground and his train of thought, centred as it was bound to be on the purpose of his journey, strayed briefly to Plummer. As an undergraduate he had scored a century before lunch here, including a six into the River Tone. Cranston had never been good at games himself, but he had an enthusiast's love of cricket as well as an admiration for those gifted at it.

He drove out on the Minehead road, past the old army camp at Norton Fitzwarren, and shortly after Bishop's Lydeard turned left towards the Brendon Hills. Slowly, almost imperceptibly, he gained height, the twin headlights probing the hedge-lined lane and revealing signposts to Combe Florey and Huish Champflower. Then, as he came to the bottom of Brendon Hill itself, the Vauxhall pointed sharply upwards, and he changed down to its lowest gear. He was on the last stage.

❧

Alone in his book-lined study, Giles Brereton went through the final draft of his Dryburgh Lecture yet again. The single desk lamp illuminated the typed pages and threw shadows into the corners of the room. He turned the pages slowly, with concentration, here and there marking with a pencil a point needing emphasis in his delivery. He came to the place where he took a sly dig at an economist rash enough to trespass in a field in which he was by no means expert and smiled thinly; then, frowning, he reread a piece about the statute of mortmain where he knew he was in an academic minefield and eventually scored out a passage he had already rephrased several times.

The action of his pencil broke his concentration. He looked across the room towards the fireplace, where a pair of logs smouldered. Above the mantelpiece a Turner watercolour, a notable member of a small but select collection, hung in shadow; beyond it, above a bookcase, the pale brown and gold of a De Wint appeared as one of the logs shifted and burst momentarily into flame. Brereton mused on the harsh existence of medieval man and his daily struggle for survival.

160

Was it any different for modern man after all? Aloud he quoted Hobbes: "Life was poor, nasty, brutish and short." As he did so his lips tightened and he thought not of the Clares, Mortimers, and Warennes in their bloodstained border castles, but of Duncan-Smith and Ashe.

He coughed and picked up his pencil again.

❧

High on the exposed uplands of Exmoor the rain closed in again, a fine drenching drizzle. At Exford, Cranston stopped for sandwiches and beer at the Crown, but was on the road again within twenty minutes. By eleven-fifteen he was at Simonsbath, a hamlet of half a dozen cottages and two hotels in the heart of the moor.

He was tired now, his eyes pricking behind his spectacles. He blinked as an approaching car failed to dip its headlights; the beat of the wipers had given him a headache. But there was not far to go. Past Goathill Bridge, through Challacombe, and up to the windswept crossroads at Blackmoor Gate; then it was downhill, a winding road, fast and deserted, to the hamlet of Kentisbury Ford. A right and left turn off the main road and half a mile down a narrow, beech-hedged lane he pulled up beside a whitewashed cottage standing by itself in a belt of trees.

He unfastened his safety belt and got out into the lane. The rain swept down drenchingly, and he was aware of a stream gurgling to one side of the cottage. The cottage itself was silent; his arrival had apparently gone unnoticed.

Pulling up his collar, he opened the white gate, brushed past an unseen bush that showered him with water, and knocked on the cottage door.

CHAPTER 21

BARNABY was awakened by the clock striking five. He lay listening to the silence that followed the last stroke, then thrust back the bedclothes and went to the window. It was still dark, and the glow of streetlamps hung over the city. Across the rooftops came the sound of a car moving up the High.

He felt the tension in himself and in the way the case was moving. The truth was that he liked cases where he sensed a growing command of the situation, where the personalities and evidence fitted a comprehensible mosaic. It did not matter if a piece or two were missing; eventually they would be found. But here there were too many imponderables. Too many motives for Ashe, too few for Duncan-Smith; too many people whose exteriors were concealing powerful emotions; too many oddities, too few connections between them. Part of his frustration was caused by the way he found himself going back to people he had previously ruled out. Take Plummer and Ferrers. Their escapade might be no more than that, but he had to recognise that there was now a dimension involving Rigby and a double link with Ashe. He wondered how disarmed he should be by Plummer's frank admissions. Again he reminded himself he was dealing with able men. What about

Wolfe, the one man without any motive at all? He had been a first-class fool—and a damned nuisance to boot—but there was nothing to give him the whiff of a motive. According to the unpredictable character of the case, that almost made him a prime suspect.

Then the two victims. Odd how one thought of them collectively—an old man and a young man with nothing in common except sudden death. Perhaps that wasn't true; perhaps he had yet to find the common factor. Could it possibly be Rigby again? He had come to see Rigby as the lynchpin of the case. That was why he had decided to visit his mother in Devon.

He was aware that he was cold. He got back into bed, his mind still flitting from one piece of unsatisfactory evidence to another. He kept returning to the phrase "Hullo, J. C." Where *was* Cranston?

Cowper and Wolfe were the last down to breakfast in the Fellows' Morning Room. They ate in silence.

At length Wolfe folded his napkin and pushed back his chair. "I'm going back to the States tomorrow, Julian."

"You're not serious? What do you mean?"

"I can't go into it all now, but the College has been good to me, and I don't want to seem ungrateful. It's all a mess, Julian. I can't concentrate on my work, I can't sleep. I'm going home. I've booked a flight."

Cowper stood up to face him. "There's more to this, Gus. What's wrong?"

"I owe you something, Julian. You've made me welcome here—you all have—but you in particular. I guess I must tell you what I told the police. I wasn't sworn to secrecy."

"This is a strange conversation."

"I was in the library."

"When?"

"I was there when the old professor was killed."

163

"You were *there?*"

"I was there. I was in the room underneath. I heard what went on upstairs. I heard . . ." Turning away from Cowper, Wolfe stared at the stone eagle perched high on the library roof. "I heard Duncan-Smith killed—and his last words. They must have been. I've told that Barnaby man."

"What did you hear?"

"He said 'Hullo, J. C.' "

Cowper leaned forward. "He said . . ."

"He called you 'J. C.' sometimes—I've heard him, Julian."

"Of course he did. And sometimes he called me 'Brereton' and 'Gibbs' and 'Farquhar.' And once he called me 'Sir Thomas' and God knows who *he* was! For Christ's sake, Gus, you don't think *I* did him in?"

"I'm not thinking anything, Julian. I'm just telling you what I heard and what I told Barnaby. And I'm going back to the States. I'll see you before I go."

Wolfe got up abruptly and left the room. Cowper ran to the door after him.

"You can't go back to the bloody States," he shouted, the mask of intellectualism slipping. "If you were there, you can't just bugger off when you feel like it. What the hell's going on in this College?"

❦

Cranston was sitting in a low-beamed room furnished with chintz, prints, and books; a fire of apple wood burned brightly; there was an atmosphere of warmth and simple good taste. Opposite him sat Mrs. Rigby, a grey-haired woman of about sixty, her delicate features dominated by wide brown eyes, her figure, tweedy and trim, still attractive. When she spoke, she looked at Cranston with affection.

"I know it's not easy, James," she said gently.

"It would be simpler if I were the only one involved."

There was another pause in what had obviously been a

desultory conversation. She leaned forward and took one of Cranston's hands in hers. "You know I want to help you, don't you?"

"Of course."

"I shall never forget what we went through over Terence. I regard our friendship as something very special. That's why I can speak as I do—no barriers. That's why I tell you, a man a hundred times cleverer than I am, what you have to do. There's no alternative."

Cranston looked at her and smiled. He squeezed her hand. "You're good for me, Mary. You always make me see myself realistically. I've come to regard you as a sort of Mother Confessor, a spiritual home if you like. You know that's why I'm here."

"I know."

"I wonder what Barnaby's thinking. He's energetic, he's turned the whole College over one way and another, but he doesn't give anything away. Not that it makes any difference. If he were to go for the wrong person, it would be even more important for me to speak out. Besides, he's no fool. He's seen the scratch"—he motioned with his arm—"he doesn't have to be a genius to get most of the way."

"Do you think anyone else guesses?"

"I shouldn't think so. For an intelligent institution, an Oxford College can be incredibly obtuse when it's faced with things it doesn't want to know. And some academic minds move in very small circles." He ran his hand over the dome of his head, as though baffled by his colleagues. "We're a curious lot. But I'm sorry to be missing Giles Brereton's Dryburgh this afternoon. He's one of the ablest of us all."

"What time are you going to leave?"

"Ever the practical one, Mary. I'll stay for lunch, if I may. Nothing much—just one of those omelettes you do so well and a touch of that Stilton I saw in the kitchen. Then I'll go back to face the music. No, that sounds too flippant. There *is* a credit side—I firmly believe that; but overall it's a terrible mess."

Mary Rigby stood up. "I'll get you a drink." She went over to his chair and touched him on the shoulder. "And I'll still be here, you know, when it's all over."

CHAPTER 22

A<small>MONG</small> scholarly Oxford occasions the Dryburgh Lecture has a unique reputation extending beyond the boundaries of its own historical discipline. Such is its drawing power over the elite of the university that it is customary for notable figures from all the humanities to foregather in the Schools to listen to a subject of which, in the very nature of things, they are themselves largely ignorant. Over the years professors of Egyptology and law have listened to analyses of such esoteric subjects as "Bastard Feudalism," "Peasant Unrest under the Tudors," and the "Significance of Tithes in the English Civil War." Historians themselves attend as a matter of course, partly out of curiosity, to see one of their eminent practitioners going through an academic hoop, and partly, no doubt, because they do not want to miss the possibility of the destruction of the reputation of one of their colleagues. This last, by no means rare in the Oxford History School, also helps to attract a substantial undergraduate audience.

The lecture was scheduled for half-past two and by this time the hall was full and noisy, the audience dressed in motley but given some semblance of uniformity by the wearing of gowns. Braine was in the front row, with Luffman on his right and Barnaby on his left. Other Beaufort Fellows, aware of the honour brought to the College by Brereton's election, had arrived early to be sure of a good seat.

Braine leaned towards Luffman. "I hope he's on form, Quentin."

"As caustic as usual, I'm sure, Master. I'm glad I'm not a fellow historian. He has rigorous standards—he once refused to read that wretched boy Grant's essays for a whole term because he kept splitting the infinitive."

The Master had donned a pair of spectacles to view the occasion more clearly. He pushed them up onto his forehead like motorcycle goggles as he turned to Barnaby. "Something to do with Welsh barons, I'm told. I never could stand the Welsh. All that frightful singing. I was once in a barrack room full of Welsh miners. They were all homesick and did nothing but sing all the time—all night and all day. I can't tell you what purgatory that was. I hope you're not Welsh?"

"No, Master. I'm a member of the rootless generation—no local loyalties at all. My mother came from East Anglia, my father was Cornish." Barnaby was impatient and already regretting having come.

"Ethnically, the Cornish are very akin to the Welsh. Ah, here's Giles, punctual as ever."

Brereton, a spare figure wearing a light grey suit and a black master's gown, took his place at the lectern. He adjusted his notes before him, and the hall fell silent. As though to check he was starting on time, he took his watch out of his waistcoat pocket, consulted it, and replaced it carefully. Then he squared his shoulders and faced the audience.

"Ladies and gentlemen, the interests of Matthew Dryburgh, in whose memory this lecture was founded, were, as many of you know, legion. Unlike his modern successors, who toil over narrow plots of land, digging ever deeper into the soil of one specialised period but knowing little of events the other side of the garden wall, Dryburgh cared for an estate of broad acres—an estate where boundaries were few and where he was prepared to deal with Greeks, Romans, Saxons, or

168

Normans on an equal basis. Frequently, of course, his tillage was shallow and there were times when his seed, broadcast without the paraphernalia of modern research, was caught in the wind of fashion and prejudice. But reading him now, none can doubt he was an historian of rare merit. He was not frightened of that hard graft which produces really detailed analysis; equally, he did not eschew the flash of imagination, the moment of vision and insight that puts a whole age into perspective—or, to return to my metaphor, gives sunlight to the uplands and shade to the valleys. It is an honour indeed to deliver the address bearing his name, standing in a line which includes Macaulay, Leopold Ranke, Samuel Rawson Gardiner, and the late John Christian Redfern, the last member of my own College to be elected.

"It is Matthew Dryburgh we remember today, and if it may be that my garden is a little narrower than his would have been, perhaps there are fewer weeds, thanks to the work of predecessors like himself. In any case, I like to think he would approve the detail of my evidence, as well as the sweep of my title—'King Edward II and the Ordainers: A Study of Patronage and Power.' "

Brereton raised his chin; his pale, fine-boned face surveyed the audience. There was a calmness, an authority about his delivery that surprised even those who knew him well. He coughed once, looked down at his notes, and then, the formalities over, launched into the main body of his text.

Barnaby, who had been eyeing some of the Beaufort Fellows in the seats round him, studied Brereton with renewed interest. Following the agrarian metaphor, he felt his own mind had been fallow. But a seed had just been planted.

Sparshott-Heyhoe was in his office dictating. He sat upright behind his desk, Miss Crisp wedged in the gap beside it. He was composing the dinner invitation being sent to old members who had agreed to help organise the Appeal.

. . . and so the Master and Fellows hope you will be able to accept the invitation to dine at the College on Founder's Day, when the Appeal manager, Brigadier Sparshott-Heyhoe, will explain the way the Appeal is being handled and how you can help Beaufort.

Yours sincerely, etc. . . .

"That's it. When you've typed that, please circulate a copy to the Master and Fellows for their approval. That's what is going out anyway, but they like to feel consulted."

He stood up and turned to the map on the wall. "Now it's back to the cards. We seem very short of men in Scotland. A laird or two would come in handy. We haven't found anyone in Galloway at all yet. Which reminds me, Miss Crisp."

"Yes, Brigadier?" She was less rubicund today, but was breathing heavily in her confined corner.

"You remember we couldn't find that card of Mr. Brereton's yesterday? Are we missing any undergraduates? We can't afford any omissions. Every penny is going to count here."

"No, I haven't found any other slips, Brigadier. It looks like a good system to me. And that card wasn't missing anyway."

"Oh?"

"No. I checked at the office when I took the cards back yesterday. One of the clerks said he took it over to the Master about a fortnight ago."

"I see." Sparshott-Heyhoe thought for a moment or two, then said, "Well, that clears it up. Now let's get back to the letter G. I want you to find out if that man Garnett is still alive. The Bursar thinks he may be playing the hermit somewhere in Cornwall. He inherited a fortune forty years ago, so he's worth doing some research on. Get hold of all the Cornish telephone directories. I'll tell you what to do next if that doesn't produce the answer."

He ignored Miss Crisp's noisy efforts to get out of her corner. He was wondering whether to tell Barnaby that Brereton's card had been sent to the Master. It was probably completely unimportant, but he had sensed Barnaby's interest.

Brereton was not disappointing his audience. After the opening courtesies, he reviewed the existing interpretations of his subject. Cool and analytical, he spared no one. An elderly female don from St. Hilda's was savaged for sentimentality in her view of Piers Gaveston; a whole school of economists was scythed down for what he regarded as a culpable misreading of the *Vita Edwardi Secundi*; and the hall was convulsed when he dismembered a sociologist who had trespassed into the Middle Ages without being able to read Latin.

With a man of lesser calibre it would have seemed cheap, the currying of favour with an intelligent but susceptible audience. As it was, the humour was incidental. Brereton was the master of his subject, and he saw no need to accord generosity to those whose scholarship fell short of their pretensions. So they were smitten hip and thigh, and ridicule is the cruellest of weapons.

Barnaby watched the performance—for performance it was —with detachment; he appreciated the humour even if the history was above his head. But he was preoccupied. Around him he could see most of the protagonists of his own drama. Braine, to his right, was smiling complacently, basking in Brereton's reflected glory. Beyond him Luffman looked serious, his face a mask of concentration. Cowper was in the row behind, but by shifting imperceptibly Barnaby could see him. Like the Master he was smiling, though in his case it was the smile of a man well-versed in the art of performance himself. Barnaby wondered what he was really like. He was either very deep or very shallow; as yet he hadn't detected a genuine emotion in him. Next to Cowper was Wolfe. He looked tired, but seemed absorbed by the lecture.

There were other Beaufort Fellows he recognised but could not put a name to. Farquhar was not there, as far as he could see. On the other side of the hall, as though distancing himself from his colleagues, Plummer was sitting with Caroline Ferrers; they both looked strained. There was no sign of Cranston.

Brereton was onto the main body of his thesis. Meticulously he analysed the politics of Edward II's reign. Details of baronial debts, land holdings, and family relationships; the avarice of the Despensers, father and son; the ruthless struggle for patronage and influence—all came under review. The prose was muted, but the argument stood out clearly. There were no jokes now; Brereton was committed to his theme, and the follies of his contemporaries were irrelevant. His audience was held, and concentration faltered only when he paused to look at his watch. He did not intend to overrun, and the exact timing of a lecture is not easy.

The grey Vauxhall pulled away from Kentisbury Ford and set off up the incline towards Exmoor. The morning sun had vanished and a pall of cloud hung over the hills. It was going to rain again.

Cranston drove carefully, yet without concentration. He thought about Brereton's Dryburgh—he would be more than halfway through by now—and about the desperate mess he was involved in. He knew what he had to do; he had always known that. But knowledge and action were two different things. He tried to imagine his interview with Barnaby.

As he did so, the horror of that night returned. Kaleidoscopically the events formed and reformed before him. And at the end the inexorable, dominating vision: the crate and the screwed-up body with its blotched and tortured face.

He drove along a shallow, wooded valley, the road straight but narrow; ahead, a shoulder of moorland loomed beyond the trees. Rain flecked the windscreen.

Why had he agreed to get involved? What a pathetic question! He would do the same again, he knew that. But the final, irrevocable decision, the moment of choice when his individuality asserted itself: What were the springs of action? He smiled sardonically. If he knew the answer to that, every historian in the business would be out of a job.

He took his hand off the wheel and looked at his watch; he hoped the lecture was going well.

❧

The applause in the hall was spontaneous and generous. There was no doubt about it; it had been an outstanding Dryburgh.

The Master took off his spectacles and put them into their case before joining in the applause. Luffman did not seem to have noticed that Brereton had finished; he was staring straight ahead. Cowper and Wolfe were clapping enthusiastically. Plummer and Ferrers were already getting up to go. Barnaby watched them all.

Brereton looked out over his audience with satisfaction, the lines of his face relaxed perceptibly. He gathered his text together, pulled his gown onto his shoulder with a nervous gesture, then moved forward to speak to the various dons who had stood up to congratulate him. This was the part he disliked—the plaudits, the congratulations. He had done the job to his satisfaction; he knew it had been good and did not need to be told. Although smiling, he withdrew into himself as the circle closed around him.

For Barnaby the moment of Brereton's triumph was the moment of his own enlightenment. As he listened to the concluding words of the lecture, the whole confused babel of fact, opinion, and surmise moved into focus. Suddenly he saw clearly what had happened and how it had happened. It did not come with the shock he expected, with that frisson of excitement that usually marked the breaking of a case. No. He found himself with a simple glow of satisfaction as he realised there could be but one answer. Dispassionately he had looked at the evidence and out of the mixture of design and chance he had produced a pattern.

What had Brereton said near the end? "The evidence available to one generation of historians has been sifted and selected by another. An historian is constantly faced with the accepted judgements of his predecessors." Barnaby knew he had been accepting judgements. *If a man lies and runs away, he must be guilty.* Cranston had lied—he knew that—and Cranston had disappeared. Therefore Cranston was guilty. Until these last few moments he had been trying to fit the facts to a prejudged theory. In the detective canon, lying and evasion equal guilt. But he hadn't waited for the facts, for the facts plain to himself, unsifted by others.

And now he had them. Now he could piece together those minutes in the library heard by Wolfe. "Hullo, J. C." slipped into place with click-pause-click-click.

He stood up and crossed to the edge of the circle round Brereton. Brereton noticed the movement and looked sharply towards him. Across the space of about five feet the eyes of the two men met, and there was an instant of communication. It was a fraction of time, as brief as the flick of an eyelid, but in that moment Barnaby saw doubt and suspicion grow to full comprehension, the comprehension that the two men shared a secret.

Looking over the shoulder of the female don in front of him, Barnaby motioned towards the door. Brereton signified his agreement.

Barnaby turned away. The audience was drifting out of the hall. He felt a touch on his arm and found Cowper at his elbow. He had the air of one wishing to impart valuable information.

"Inspector, I don't want to get involved in this business more than I have to, but you ought to know that Wolfe is planning to go back to the States."

"When?"

"Tomorrow. He's got a ticket. I've told him he can't, but . . ."

Barnaby cut in. "Where is he?"

"He was here a moment ago. I think he's gone back to Beaufort."

"Get hold of him and don't let him out of your sight." Barnaby was curt to the point of rudeness; his trained deference had dissolved in the tension of the moment.

He turned to look at Brereton again. But the group around him had broken up. Brereton had gone.

CHAPTER 23

BARNABY went straight back to Beaufort. The complacency of the last few minutes had given way to an apprehension he recognised from his early days as an inexperienced constable. What if it all went wrong now? All so clear, all so simple, and yet . . .

At the Lodge Barker was waiting for him. "Mr. Brereton said you'd be coming, sir. Said 'e'd wait for you in the chapel."

"The chapel?" Apprehension was replaced by perplexity.

"Yes, sir. He said you 'ad an understanding to meet after 'is lecture. He thought you'd not be interrupted there. He's a bit of a celebrity today and 'e was finding it 'ard to shake people off when 'e got back just now."

Barnaby walked to the chapel; his legs, moving in their curious way, covered the ground in ungainly strides. He opened the door and went in. The chapel appeared deserted. On each side the tiered oak pews ranged backwards to the elaborately carved stalls reserved for the Fellows. The nave was in shadow; in the chancel a shaft of sunlight cut across the choir, sharpening the contrast between the black and white tiles on the floor.

"Up here, Inspector." The voice was unmistakably Brereton's. "Up here, by the organ."

Barnaby looked up at the organ pipes climbing to the roof to the right of the rood screen. The voice remained disembodied, in that setting sepulchral.

"Come to the chancel steps, Inspector. Look to your right and you'll see a door."

The tone was peremptory and Barnaby resented it. Nevertheless, he did as he'd been told. He went through the door and found himself at the bottom of a narrow spiral staircase. Gingerly, because there was precious little light, he started up it. Twice around the central stone column and he emerged into the organ loft. It was empty.

"Keep climbing, Barnaby. I don't think we want to be disturbed." The voice was still above him.

Barnaby went back to the stairs, which continued to spiral upwards in the wall of the chapel. Two more turns and from a low Gothic arch he stepped out onto the roof of one of the side aisles. To his right was a low balustrade and a sheer drop to Fletcher Quad; ahead was another door, giving access to a fanciful tower decorated with elaborate Victorian pinnacles and curlicues.

"It's quiet here. We shan't be disturbed."

He looked up and saw Brereton standing inside a low parapet a few feet above him just the other side of the tower. He had taken off his gown but otherwise looked as composed as when giving the lecture.

"It was good of you to wait until I'd finished. We'll talk with this distance between us to start with, if you don't mind."

"I believe we understood each other just now, sir."

"I believe we did. May I ask how long you've known?"

"Since this afternoon. You finally told me yourself. I don't suppose you know it yet, but Wolfe was in the basement of the library that night. He heard a good deal of what went on, including Duncan-Smith saying, 'Hullo, J. C.' Do you remember that? To start with that pushed me towards Cranston or Cowper. But you and I know who it was, don't we?"

Brereton was leaning forward intently, one foot on the parapet; behind him the cupola of the College clock poked upwards from the Lodge. He said nothing.

"Professor Duncan-Smith made mistakes, but there was usually a logic of his own behind them. When he saw you in the library that night, he called you 'J. C.' because he had known the last Dryburgh lecturer as J. C.—the John Christian Redfern to whom you paid such eloquent tribute this afternoon. I'd already heard the name Redfern, but had no idea of the initials until you gave them to me. Time stood still for Duncan-Smith. He knew you had been elected to the Dryburgh, but he saw you as J. C. Redfern, the man on whose staircase he had once lived. And then his time stopped altogether because you killed him."

Brereton's head pulled back sharply. "It was an accident. I had nothing against the old man."

"Tell me about it." Barnaby felt uneasy about this interview being conducted nearly fifty feet above the ground amid gargoyles and flying buttresses, but he sensed a tension in Brereton that warned him to make no challenge for the time being. "Suppose you start at the beginning, sir."

"Very well. To start at the very beginning, I decided a long time ago that anyone who killed David Ashe would be doing a public service. I thought quite seriously about doing it myself, but as an intelligent being I knew I'd be caught. Even the removal of a creature like Ashe was not worth a lifetime in prison. Then, suddenly, everything changed—to be accurate, two things changed.

"First, there was the manuscript. From the start I suspected Ashe. Then on Wednesday, just before my talk at the freshmen's dinner, he came to my rooms. 'Going to indoctrinate all those poor green sods with the history of the College, are you?' he said. 'Show them what a real world thinks of your elitist hogwash.' And he threw down the bits of the letter on the floor. He'd gone before I could say anything. But I knew then I was going to kill him. I didn't know how

178

or when, but I was certain. I'd never seen such a calculated piece of nihilism."

"And the other thing?"

"Was personal. I've been seeing my doctor for the past fortnight and on Tuesday I had the result of some tests. No doubt you can guess the outcome. Yes, I see you can. Pulmonary fibrosis—I've got nine months at the outside."

A breeze ruffled Brereton's hair. The pale sun threw his shadow up the leaded roof of the chapel. From the far side of the quad the laugh of a girl floated upwards.

"Nine months, Inspector. Not long, but long enough for what I had to do. And now it didn't matter whether I was caught or not. I took no real precautions. Just seized the chance when it came. No planning in the true sense of the word. That night I knew he was in the library, and when I thought he was alone I went straight in and killed him. Doesn't that sound simple?"

"Did you speak to him?"

"No. There had to be no mistake, I was giving him no chances. No, I waited till he was absorbed in his reading and then I had the tie round his neck before he could cry out. He struggled, of course, and he was stronger than he looked—we probably all are, Inspector, when we know it's life or death. He managed to get up and he pulled a whole set of books down when he was flailing about, but he hadn't a chance. And in those final seconds I'm glad to say he knew it. When he eventually went limp, I had the most enormous satisfaction, the sense of a job well done."

Brereton paused and stood back a little. He looked down at the foreshortened figures in the quadrangle. A chattering party of tourists was being guided to the main door of the chapel.

Barnaby tried to take stock of the situation. He was alarmed by the calmness of Brereton's manner. It was assured, confident, almost as though he was continuing his lecture; the manner of a man who was in command, who

179

knew exactly what he was doing. By contrast Barnaby felt ineffectual, as though events were slipping away from him. He, too, looked down into the quadrangle and his imagination recoiled at the thought of a fall from that height. He looked back at Brereton, trying to judge the distance between them. A hazardous jump, even for a young man . . .

Brereton was speaking again. "I tidied up the books—I gather not very effectively. Then I discovered I was not alone. As I came out of the bay, the old man came round the corner from the bay next door. 'Hullo, J. C.,' he said, and I lost my temper. It's strange, but in retrospect I can analyse my emotions very clearly. When I killed Ashe, I was cold and clinical: a job had to be done: it was almost an academic exercise. Then Duncan-Smith came blundering in and my emotions—which had somehow been suspended while I was dealing with Ashe—overflowed. I was angry that he was there, angry with myself for not checking beforehand, and irritated beyond belief by 'Hullo, J. C.' I just grabbed him and shook him. He didn't say anything, but his mouth fell open in that senile way of his—and just for a second I realised that this wreck of a being who had been dying on his feet for years would probably live longer than I would. That's when it happened. I pushed him away roughly, and he fell with his head against the bookcase. Within seconds I realised I had killed him too. It was inexcusable."

The last words were clipped, a total condemnation devoid of self-pity.

"I'd just realised there was nothing I could do for him when the library door opened and Cranston came in. It was an extraordinary scene. There was I, Senior Fellow, pillar of rectitude, with two bodies; there was he, huffing and puffing, a caricature of horror and astonishment. I told him what had happened—we whispered, I remember, though we had no idea anyone else was there—and asked him to help me. He agreed, very reluctantly—poor man, I didn't give him much chance to think. For reasons of his own, which he may have told you, he disliked Ashe as much as most of us did. But I want to make it clear I persuaded him against his will.

"Together we put Duncan-Smith back at the table; together we stuffed Ashe's body into one of the book crates and carried it out to my car through the postern. For two elderly men we didn't do badly in terms of time. But Cranston wouldn't help me get rid of the body. He said he had an appointment with the Master. In any case, by the time he'd helped pick up two bodies he was beginning to have second thoughts about getting involved at all." Brereton almost smiled. "I think that's an understatement, Inspector. I think he bitterly regretted it. He is, fundamentally, a man of complete integrity, whatever tittle-tattle you may have heard.

"When Cranston left, I went back to the library to tidy up. I picked up the books and had a last look around. I'd no idea, of course, that Wolfe was in the basement."

"You did something else."

"Oh?"

"You looked at your watch—twice. Wolfe heard a metallic sound: click-pause-click-click. I couldn't identify it until you opened and shut your watch during your lecture this afternoon. That was when I really knew. I couldn't hear it, but I could see the rhythm and it's quite unmistakable."

Brereton inclined his head. "Well done, Inspector. And I hope that doesn't sound patronising. It's not meant to."

"What did you do with Ashe?"

"I think you know that. I'd made no plans, no preparations, and once Cranston had gone I was on my own. I drove to the one place where I thought a crate might go unnoticed for a while. When I got to the station, it was late and there were very few people around. But just the other side of the railway bridge there's a rough little park which collects the local drunks. It was a risk, of course, but I found one who could stand upright and offered him a tip if he would help with the crate. He had no idea what was in it, and together we lifted it out of my car and carried it up the ramp to the

181

freight department. The sliding door was open and no one was around so we just pushed the crate in. I gave the man a fiver and reckoned that with what he'd got on board already he wouldn't remember much in the morning. It was as simple as that."

"Why did you use the tie?"

Barnaby wanted an answer, but he knew he was really playing for time. He sensed an increase in tension as his question interrupted the donnish exposition. Brereton stared at him.

"The trouble with Western society, Inspector, is that it's lost its will. Read your Solzhenitsyn. We've got our freedoms, but the threats to them are all around—and we don't recognise them when we see them. Liberty is confused with licence everywhere; pallid liberals encourage anarchy and then hold up their hands in pious horror when it happens. We're an open society, naive and gullible, and hopelessly vulnerable to the dedicated fanatic. Men like Ashe are the worm in the bud; the harm they do is incalculable. I killed him with a Beaufort tie as a pathetic gesture of defiance, to show that the heritage of which Beaufort is part has the guts to defend itself. An atavistic response—simple self-preservation. Duncan-Smith was a tragedy. I would kill Ashe again. He and his kind want to destroy a whole culture. A man who could tear up a priceless manuscript . . ."

"You put the remains in the post when Ashe was dead?" asked Barnaby, trying to lower the emotional temperature.

"Fill in the details yourself, Inspector. I just wish I'd done it earlier before he'd affected others—like Rigby. Do you know why Cranston helped me? I'll tell you. Because he once did his damnedest to save Rigby. He spent hours trying to lift the shroud that man had cast over him. Quite unavailingly, of course, but he discovered the damage one human being can do to another in the interest of a warped ideology. Revolution—the new paganism, Cranston called it. When I found I had a time limit on my life, I knew what I had to do."

182

Barnaby was near enough to see how tightly the skin stretched across the bones of Brereton's face.

"Our civilisation is at stake and we don't realise it. Surely you can see that we have to defend all this?" He waved an arm in a gesture embracing all the spires and towers of Oxford. "You're an intelligent man, Inspector. Someone has to make a stand."

"And what about the rule of law?" Barnaby dropped his official deference. "Isn't that part of our civilisation? What would happen if every individual took the law into his own hands and disposed of those he disapproved of?"

Brereton seemed to be irritated by the unexpected challenge. He pulled away and walked to the far end of the roof. Barnaby, who was more concerned with getting Brereton and himself back to the safety of firm ground than with a philosophical dispute, immediately saw his chance. He moved quickly to the door in the turret, opened it, and crossed to the other roof. He found himself inside the parapet on a ledge barely two feet wide. On one side the slope of the roof climbed upwards; on the other there was a sheer drop to the quadrangle. Brereton was just over a yard away.

"I think we should go down, Mr. Brereton."

Brereton turned to face him. He appeared not to notice that he had changed his position, and he totally ignored what Barnaby said.

"Let's go down, sir."

"Why?"

As he spoke, Brereton put out a hand onto the roof to steady himself. It was an unremarkable gesture and in normal circumstances would have gone unnoticed. But for Barnaby it was the significant moment when Brereton's self-assurance wavered. Quite suddenly he saw a simple truth. This scholarly man whose academic prowess had so recently made him feel an intellectual pygmy wanted *his* approval. His belief in his own rightness was undented, but he wanted the emotional prop of an ordinary man's support—and he, Barnaby, could not give it.

"You're too intelligent, Mr. Brereton, to need me to justify the law. But I will say this. I can't approve of what you did, but I think I begin to understand you. Now please come down. I don't know about you, but I haven't much of a head for heights."

Brereton did not move. He said: "You *must* see. You must see that in the end someone has to act . . ."

"If you come now, sir, you'll be able to explain to everyone." Barnaby took a calculated risk. He turned his back and went to the door.

Brereton put his hand on the roof again and when he spoke his voice was gentler than before. "All right, Inspector, though I did expect you to understand—you of all people."

Barnaby savoured the moment; he felt elation and relief rising within him in equal proportions. He turned to watch Brereton come towards him.

What happened next seemed to take place in slow motion. Brereton took a couple of steps forward, but stumbled in a narrow rain gutter running across the roof. He fell forwards and to save himself threw out a hand against the parapet to his left. Barnaby watched helplessly as the stonework gave way under the sudden impact and Brereton's whole weight was thrust against the parapet. This was too much for the soot-encrusted sandstone and before he could recover his balance Brereton rolled sideways off the roof. Accompanied by falling masonry, arms and legs flailing, he fell into space. Halfway down he struck a buttress and uttered a brief cry as he was deflected outwards. An instant later he was a crumpled puppet on the steps leading down to the crypt.

Barnaby looked over the edge and then he was moving before he really comprehended what had happened. Clumsily, disjointedly, he ran down the endless stairs, through the organ loft, past the tourists in the chapel, and out into the sunlight.

Barker was there before him, bending over Brereton. He straightened up as Barnaby approached.

"It's no good, sir," he said. " 'E's gone."

There was no more to say. Barnaby stood by the broken body while Barker fetched a blanket from the Lodge. Amidst a host of emotions, Barnaby found himself wondering, absurdly, whether Luffman might use the collapse of the parapet as evidence that the chapel should take priority in the Appeal.

The day afterwards, Barnaby spoke to Cranston privately before seeing the other Fellows. Cranston had admitted his part in the affair and was recovering his aplomb.

"It's difficult to say what makes a man act irrevocably, Inspector." Cranston's tone was didactic. "When he told me he had only a few months, he was a changed man. But the destruction of the manuscript was crucial. When we talked in the library that night, the letter was in the forefront of his mind. He kept going back to it."

"Whereas with you it was Rigby."

"Quite so—that and the telephone persecution. I didn't have the sort of relationship with Rigby that everyone suspected. It was nothing like Burgess. No, I just had immense compassion for him when I saw the way a scholarly mind was being seduced. Cowper should have done more for him, but he was too tied up with his own self-centred affairs. I got to know him and his mother well during the crises he went through and, in a curious way, his mother has become my closest friend. Which is why, of course, I went down to see her."

"I thought Rigby was more central to the case than he proved."

"I'm not surprised. The smell of that business permeated the College."

"The file misled me. I was convinced its disappearance was

185

significant, but I discovered this morning that the Master's still got it. He didn't return it after the decision to end Rigby's Fellowship."

"I did warn you, Inspector. I rather doubt if any donnish system is foolproof when it comes to administrative details. Not our strength, you might say."

"The Master's got Brereton's card, too. I gather he sent for it when he was writing a piece about him for some magazine after his election to the Dryburgh."

"He always checks his details."

"You realise, Professor, that your own contribution to all this cannot be overlooked."

Cranston inclined his head. "I understand that. There will be no more concealment now. I want to minimise the effects on the College. I'm not sure how my colleagues will react when they hear the whole truth. Some of them are more erratic in their normal state than Giles ever became."

❧

Later that evening Barnaby joined the resident Fellows in the Senior Common Room for coffee after Hall. They were all there except Cranston, who had decided to stay away.

It was a gloomy gathering, and even the Master's capacity for cheerfulness in the face of adversity was being tested. When Barnaby had finished expounding the case, Plummer circulated with the coffeepot.

"It was for the best," said Luffman. He was for once wearing his clerical collar and, paradoxically, looking more relaxed.

"Theologically unsound," said Braine. "I would not have expected the Church to take such a pragmatic view."

"Mother Church is very flexible," interposed Cowper, who could never resist a dig at religion. "I've been asked to do a programme called 'The Survival of Christianity.' Perhaps you could give me a hand, Quentin?"

"Well, Brigadier, when do we start the Appeal?" asked Braine tactfully, turning to Sparshott-Heyhoe.

"We can't delay any longer, Master. Assuming there are no more harmful revelations to come, I think we should arrange the Launch at the end of next week. Frankly," he added lugubriously, "I have never handled a job where the omens have been worse."

Braine looked around the circle of chairs and caught Farquhar's eye. He coughed and looked mischievous. "Er—there is one thing I should tell you, gentlemen. You may recall that there was some talk about the College having an interest in Professor Duncan-Smith's will. I believe it may even have been suggested to you, Brigadier, that his contribution might be used as a sort of publicity 'starter' to show how an old Beaufort man remembered his alma mater with loyalty and gratitude." Braine took a sip of coffee, relishing the moment. "I regret to have to tell you that our late colleague had a little more life in him than we gave him credit for. There is apparently a lady in Slough with certain physical attractions who gave some solace to his declining years and who is the sole beneficiary under his will. I believe she is the richer—and we the poorer—by a substantial sum, about a hundred and fifty thousand pounds."

He turned to Sparshott-Heyhoe. "So I very much fear, Brigadier, that we do not even qualify for a consolation prize."